The Cartoon Chronicles of America

FIGHT FOR FREEDOM

ALSO BY STAN MACK AND SUSAN CHAMPLIN

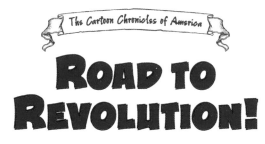

The Cartoon Chronicles of America

ROAD TO REVOLUTION!

The Cartoon Chronicles of America

FIGHT FOR FREEDOM

Stan Mack and Susan Champlin

BLOOMSBURY

NEW YORK BERLIN LONDON SYDNEY

First published in the United States of America in July 2012
by Bloomsbury Books for Young Readers
www.bloomsburykids.com

For information about permission to reproduce selections from this book, write to
Permissions, Bloomsbury BFYR, 175 Fifth Avenue, New York, New York 10010

Library of Congress Cataloging-in-Publication Data
Mack, Stanley.
Fight for freedom / by Stan Mack and Susan Champlin. — 1st U.S. ed.
p. cm. — (The cartoon chronicles of America)
Summary: In 1861, a young slave named Sam escapes to search for his father, who has been conscripted into the Confederate Army, and makes his way to a northern city, while back at the Virginia plantation where Sam was raised, Annabelle, the owner's daughter, struggles to run things after her father's death.
ISBN 978-1-59990-835-9 (paperback) · ISBN 978-1-59990-014-8 (hardcover)
1. Graphic novels. [1. Graphic novels. 2. Slavery—Fiction. 3. Plantation life—Virginia—Fiction. 4. Virginia—History—Civil War, 1861-1865—Fiction. 5. United States—History—Civil War, 1861-1865—Fiction.] I. Champlin, Susan. II. Title.
PZ7.7.M33Fig 2012 741.5'973—dc23 2011040481

Typeset in CCFaceFont
Art created with Pigma Micron pen and Pelikan watercolor on 1-ply Strathmore paper
Book design by Stan Mack, Susan Champlin, and Yelena Safronova

Printed in China by Hung Hing Printing (China) Co., Ltd., Shenzhen, Guangdong
2 4 6 8 10 9 7 5 3 1 (paperback)
2 4 6 8 10 9 7 5 3 1 (hardcover)

All papers used by Bloomsbury Publishing, Inc., are natural, recyclable products made from wood grown in well-managed forests. The manufacturing processes conform to the environmental regulations of the country of origin.

For Susan's parents: Peggy Champlin, PhD, for her enthusiastic and scholarly support of our books, and Charles Champlin, for his brilliant insights into the art and craft of writing

The Cartoon Chronicles of America

FIGHT FOR FREEDOM

PROLOGUE

IN WHICH WE LEARN HOW WE GOT HERE

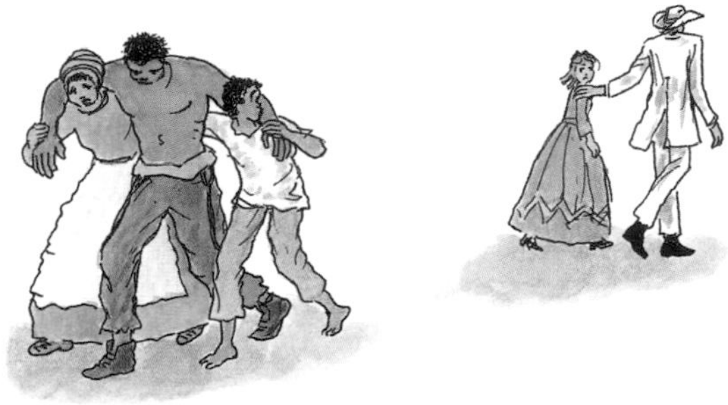

Of all the issues that led to the Civil War, one overshadowed every other: slavery.

Slavery was nothing new in the 1800s. In fact, slavery had existed throughout history, including in ancient Greece and Egypt. And when traders brought the first shipload of Africans to Virginia in the early 1600s, slavery took hold in the new colonies.

The Declaration of Independence claimed that "all men are created equal"—but several Founding Fathers owned slaves. The signers of the Constitution meant to form "a more perfect Union"—but accepted slavery as a fact of life.

By the early 1800s, the North and South were very different places. The North had bustling cities, busy factories, and many people, white and black, who believed that slavery was immoral and must be "abolished" (gotten rid of). These people were called "abolitionists."

The South was largely rural and agricultural, with a smaller population. Using slave labor allowed plantation owners to enjoy wealth and leisure. Citizens of Southern states believed they had a constitutional right to keep slaves and hated outsiders telling them what they could and couldn't do.

As the country expanded West, new territories meant new battlegrounds over slavery. A series of events inflamed the issue. These included the Fugitive Slave Act (which said that citizens were required to help capture and return escaped slaves) and the Supreme Court's Dred Scott decision, which said that people of African descent could never be citizens (and therefore had no legal rights) and said that the federal government did not have the power to prohibit slavery in the territories.

Abolitionists were outraged. Many helped slaves run away through the Underground Railroad, a secret network of escape routes to the free states and Canada. The issue of slavery now divided the country: North versus South, abolitionist versus slave owner, states' righters versus those who believed in federal government control. Some were even demanding the country's breakup.

In 1860, Abraham Lincoln was elected president of the United States. Although he said he would not interfere with slavery in the states in which it already existed, Southerners believed that he meant to abolish slavery.

On December 20, 1860, South Carolina left the union—or "seceded"—soon followed by Mississippi, Florida, Alabama, Georgia, Louisiana, and Texas. Together they formed the Confederate States of America.

Lincoln declared that no state on its own could choose to leave the union. On April 12, 1861, the Confederate states bombarded Fort Sumter, the federal fort in the port of Charleston, South Carolina. The troops in the fort surrendered. The Civil War had officially begun.

Four days later, Virginia, Arkansas, North Carolina, and Tennessee seceded. Northerners and Southerners rushed into uniform—each side believing the war would be short-lived.

The first important battle took place at Manassas Junction, Virginia, in July 1861, twenty-five miles southwest of Washington City (now called Washington, DC). The Rebels sent the Yanks running, but it was clear that both sides needed organizing, training, and discipline.

The federals devised a two-part plan. In the West, the goal was to gain control of the Mississippi River. In the East, it was to capture Richmond, Virginia, the capital of the Confederacy. During the course of the war, more fighting would take place in Virginia than in any other state.

In the spring of 1862, the Union Army of the Potomac began pushing toward Richmond from the coast, only to be stopped by a smaller Confederate force, led by the man who would become the South's greatest general: Robert E. Lee. The war then moved from the outskirts of Richmond to northern Virginia.

Our story opens at Twin Oaks, a small plantation just south of Fredericksburg, Virginia. It is July 1862, and the war is coming ever closer to Twin Oaks's doorstep...

In this book, you'll meet fictional characters who get caught up with real-life people and events. After reading our story, please turn to the epilogue, in the back. There, you'll find out what's fact and what's fiction.

THE MAIN CHARACTERS

ABRAHAM LINCOLN

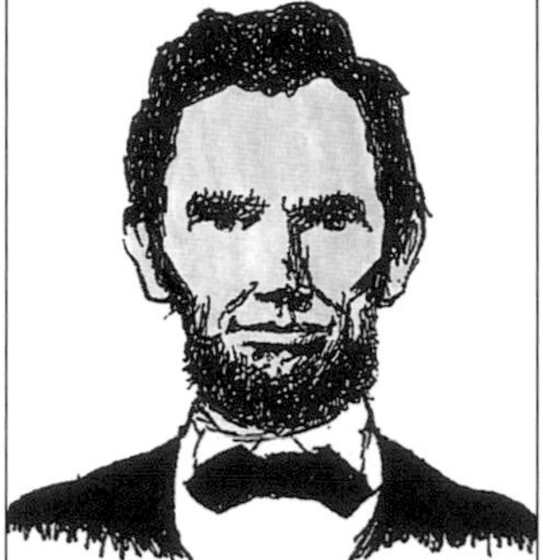

President of the United States during the Civil War.

JOHNNY REB & BILLY YANK

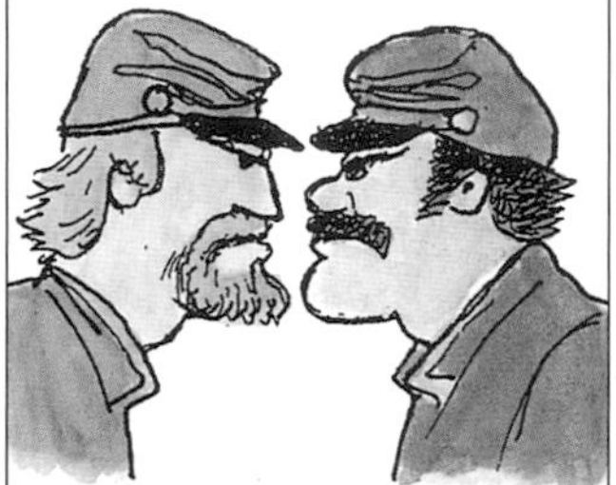

Nicknames for Confederate and Union soldiers.

EZEKIEL "ZEKE" JEFFERSON

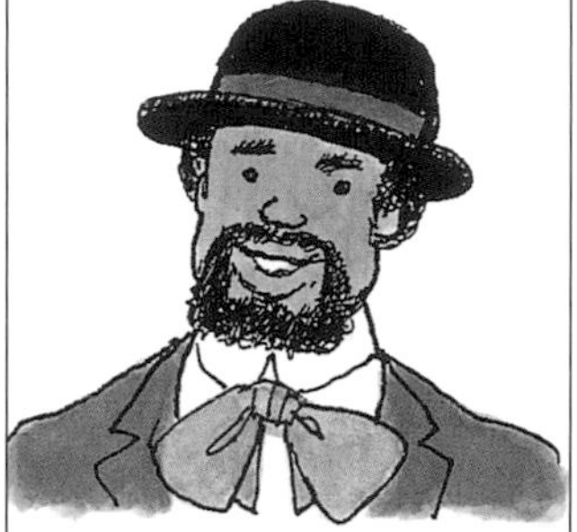

An African American reporter covering the war for the North.

CAROLINE & BEAUMONT "BEAU" BEAUREGARD

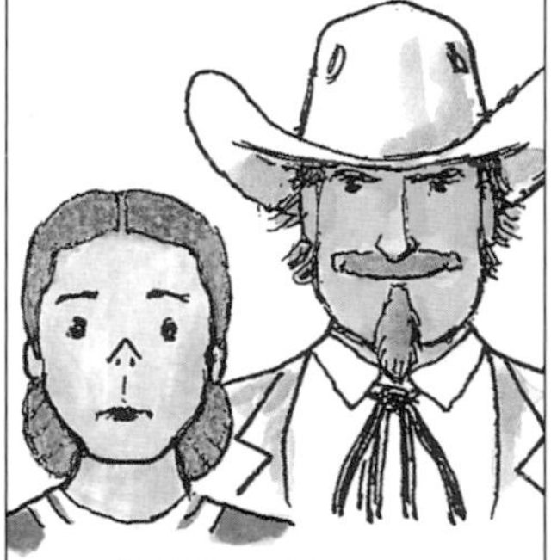

Mistress and master of Twin Oaks Plantation.

MAE & JOSEPH

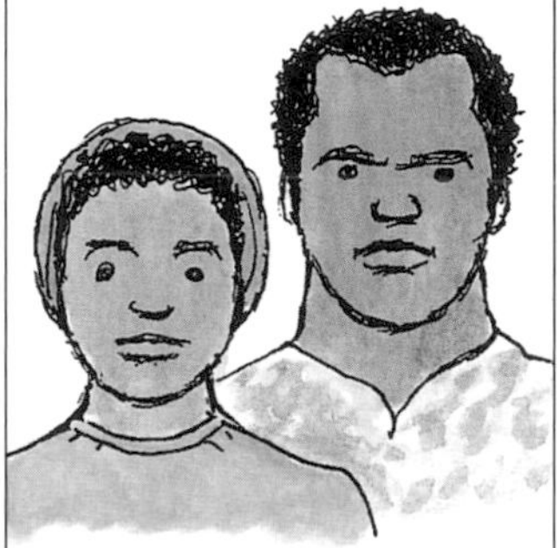

Mae is Caroline's personal slave. Joseph is a field slave at Twin Oaks.

MR. TWIST

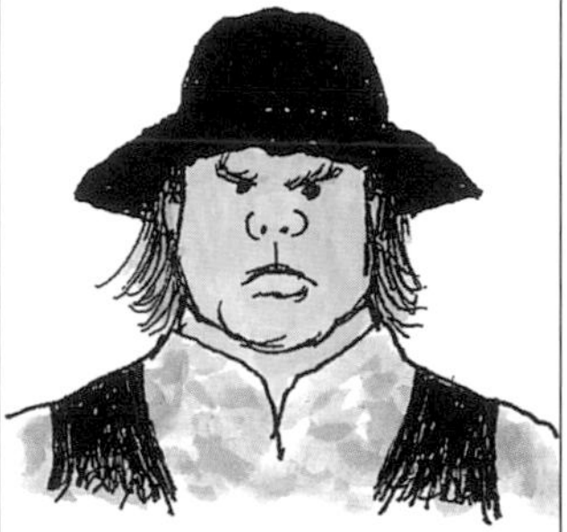

The Twin Oaks overseer.

SAM

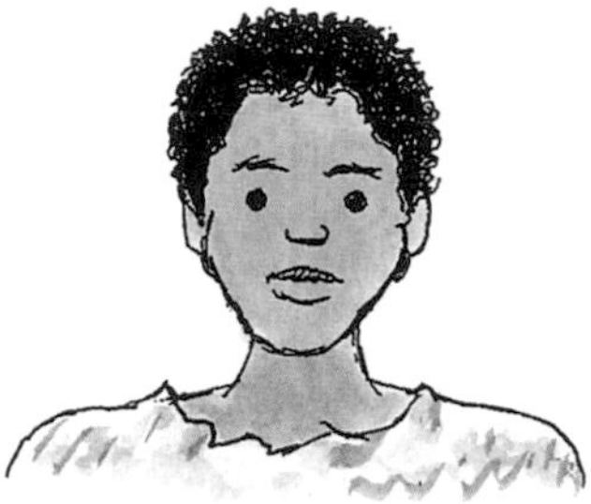

Young house slave at Twin Oaks Plantation. Son of Mae and Joseph. Sam is the same age as Annabelle Beauregard.

ANNABELLE BEAUREGARD

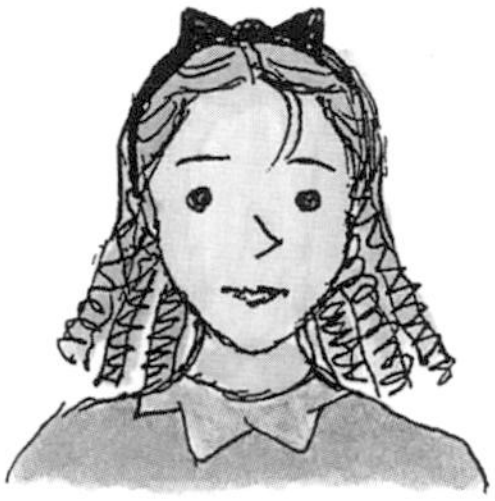

Daughter of Caroline and Beau. As a young child, Annabelle was cared for by Mae and played with Sam. But their worlds are changing.

TWIN OAKS PLANTATION

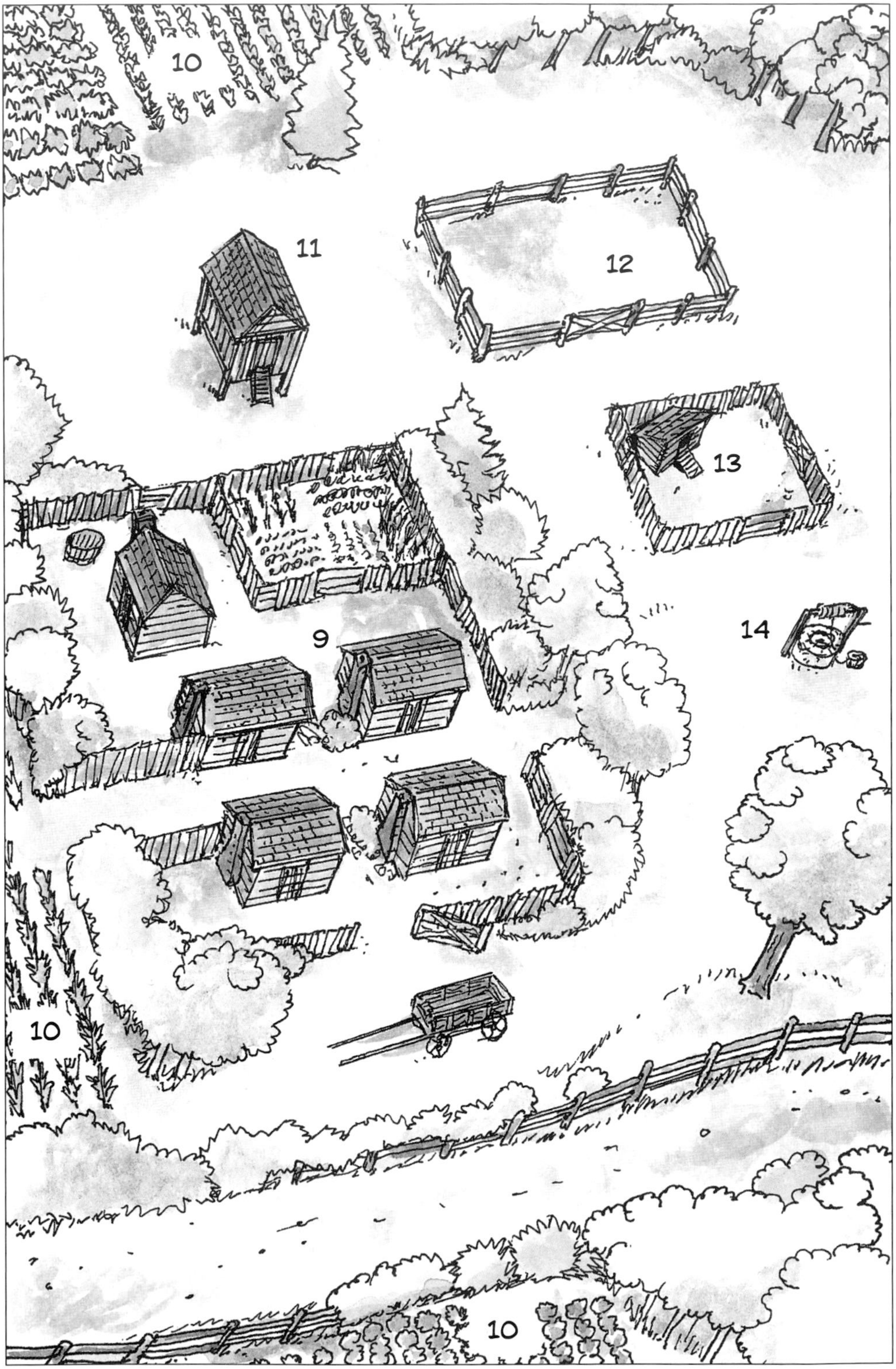
10
11
12
13
9
14
10
10

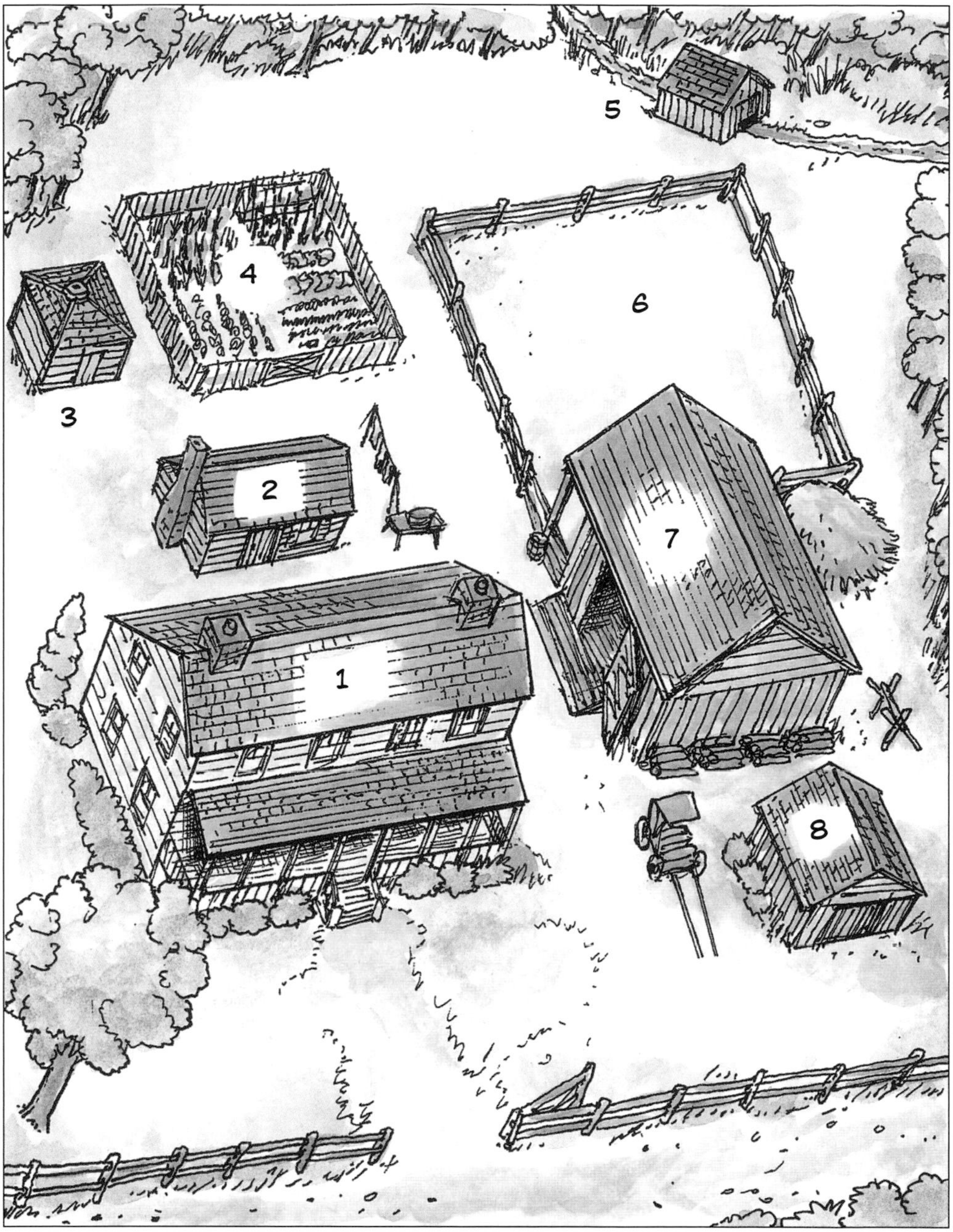
5
4
6
3
2
7
1
8

1. MAIN HOUSE
2. KITCHEN
3. SMOKEHOUSE
4. GARDEN
5. SPRINGHOUSE
6. CORRAL
7. BARN
8. CARRIAGE HOUSE
9. SLAVE QUARTERS
10. THE FIELDS
11. CORNCRIB
12. SHEEP PEN
13. HENHOUSE
14. WELL

VIRGINIA & WASHINGTON CITY, 1862

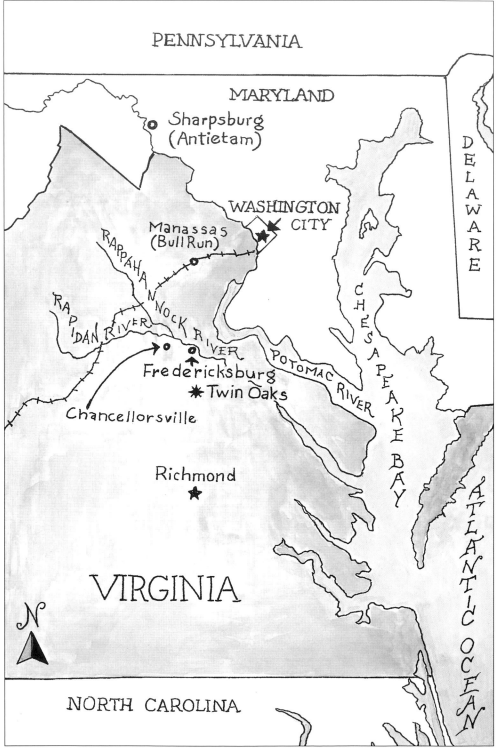

PENNSYLVANIA

MARYLAND

Sharpsburg
(Antietam)

DELAWARE

WASHINGTON CITY

Manassas
(Bull Run)

RAPPAHANNOCK RIVER

RAPIDAN RIVER

POTOMAC RIVER

CHESAPEAKE BAY

Fredericksburg

Twin Oaks

Chancellorsville

Richmond

VIRGINIA

N

ATLANTIC OCEAN

NORTH CAROLINA

CHAPTER 1

The Confederate Army, commanded by General Robert E. Lee, has beaten back every attack into Virginia by the Union forces. Each new assault serves only to inspire more devotion in the South.

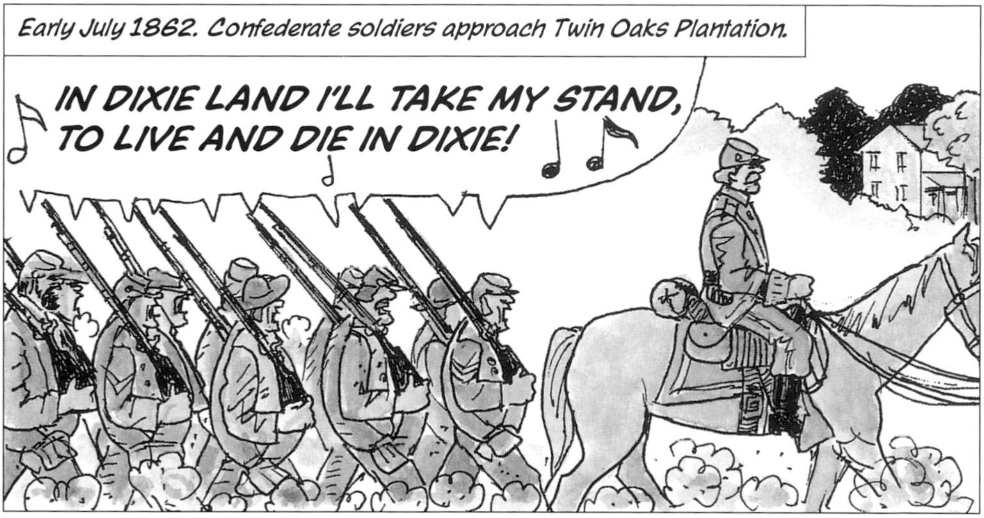
Early July 1862. Confederate soldiers approach Twin Oaks Plantation.
IN DIXIE LAND I'LL TAKE MY STAND, TO LIVE AND DIE IN DIXIE!

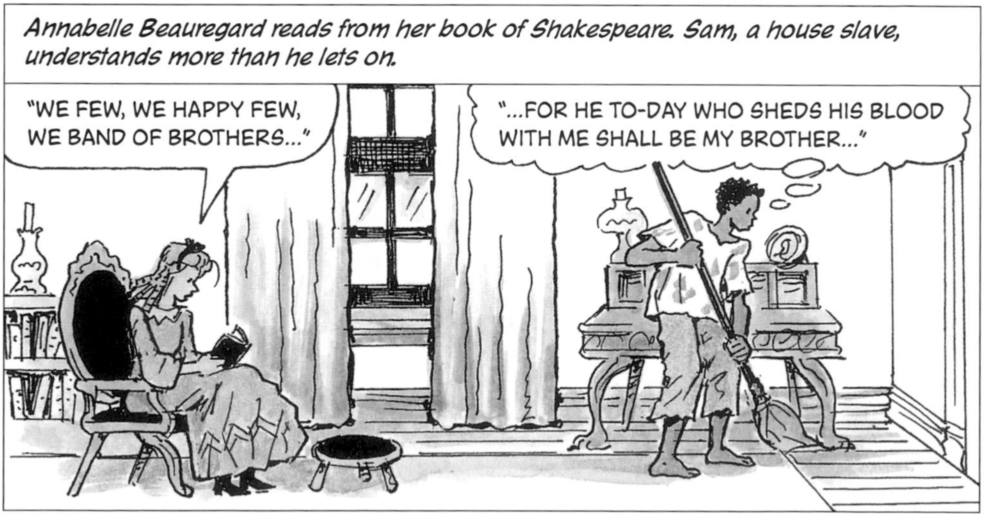
Annabelle Beauregard reads from her book of Shakespeare. Sam, a house slave, understands more than he lets on.
"WE FEW, WE HAPPY FEW, WE BAND OF BROTHERS..."
"...FOR HE TO-DAY WHO SHEDS HIS BLOOD WITH ME SHALL BE MY BROTHER..."

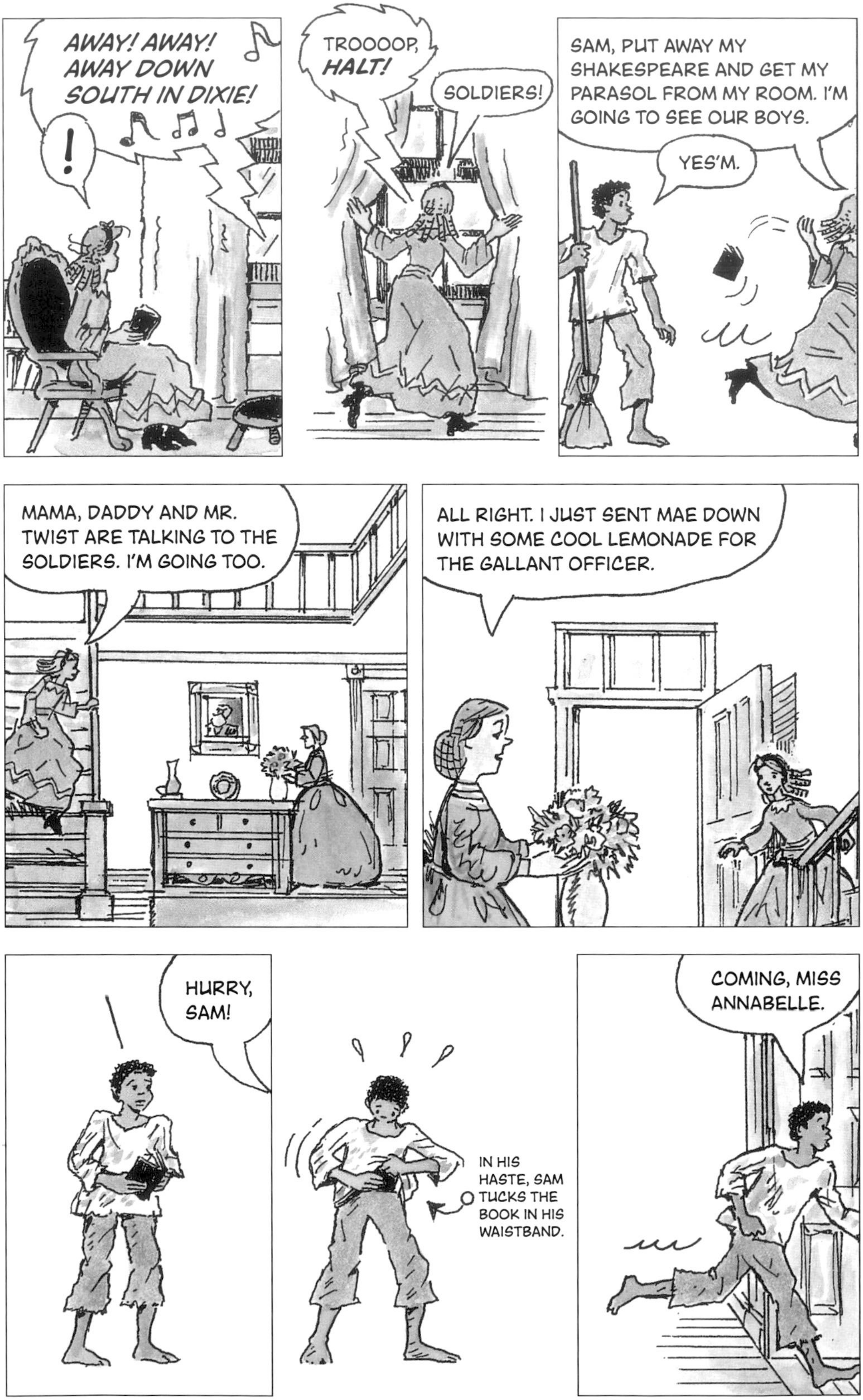
AWAY! AWAY! AWAY DOWN SOUTH IN DIXIE!
!
TROOOOP, HALT!
SOLDIERS!
SAM, PUT AWAY MY SHAKESPEARE AND GET MY PARASOL FROM MY ROOM. I'M GOING TO SEE OUR BOYS.
YES'M.
MAMA, DADDY AND MR. TWIST ARE TALKING TO THE SOLDIERS. I'M GOING TOO.
ALL RIGHT. I JUST SENT MAE DOWN WITH SOME COOL LEMONADE FOR THE GALLANT OFFICER.
HURRY, SAM!
IN HIS HASTE, SAM TUCKS THE BOOK IN HIS WAISTBAND.
COMING, MISS ANNABELLE.

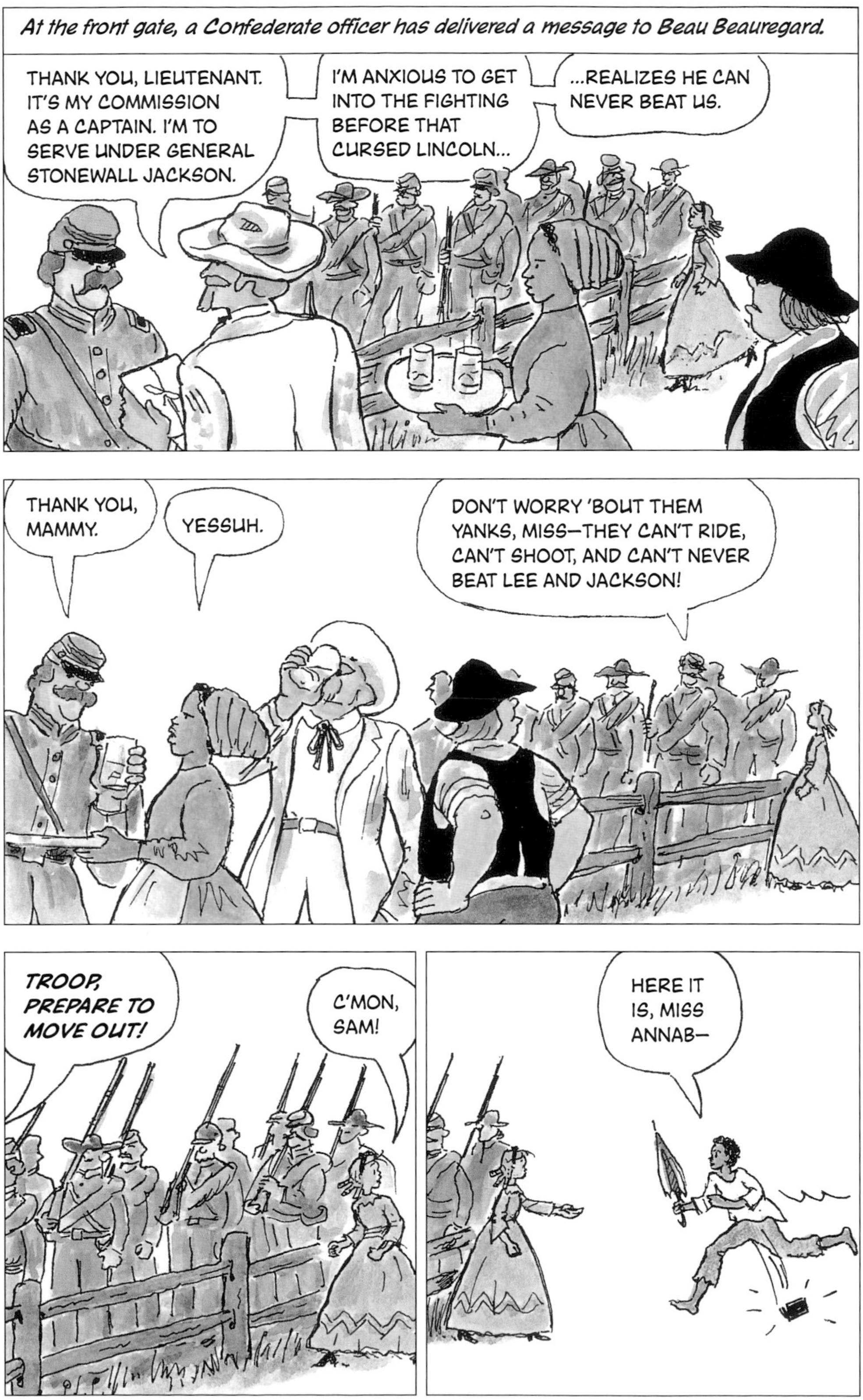
At the front gate, a Confederate officer has delivered a message to Beau Beauregard.
THANK YOU, LIEUTENANT. IT'S MY COMMISSION AS A CAPTAIN. I'M TO SERVE UNDER GENERAL STONEWALL JACKSON.
I'M ANXIOUS TO GET INTO THE FIGHTING BEFORE THAT CURSED LINCOLN...
...REALIZES HE CAN NEVER BEAT US.
THANK YOU, MAMMY.
YESSUH.
DON'T WORRY 'BOUT THEM YANKS, MISS—THEY CAN'T RIDE, CAN'T SHOOT, AND CAN'T NEVER BEAT LEE AND JACKSON!
TROOP, PREPARE TO MOVE OUT!
C'MON, SAM!
HERE IT IS, MISS ANNAB—

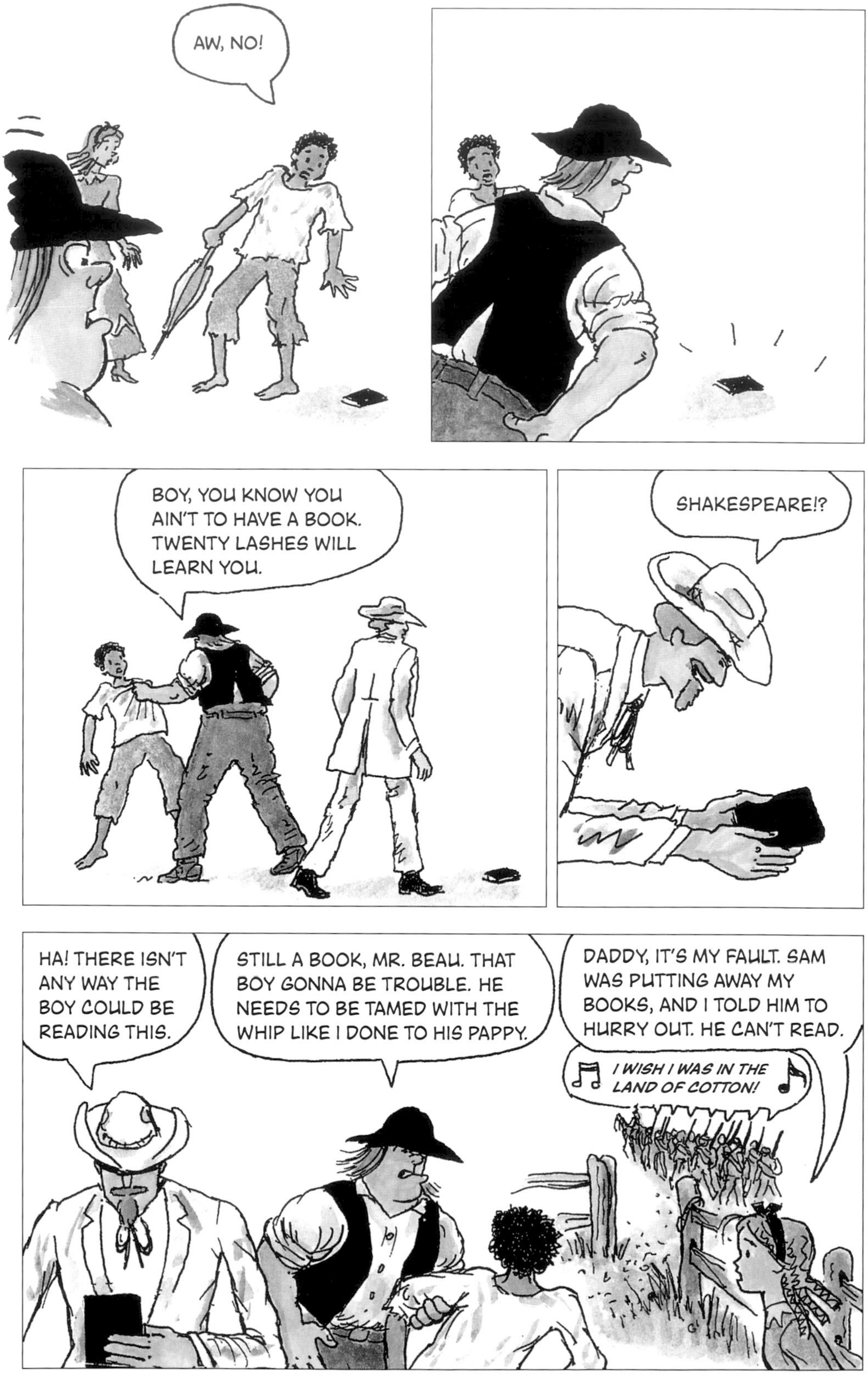
AW, NO!
BOY, YOU KNOW YOU AIN'T TO HAVE A BOOK. TWENTY LASHES WILL LEARN YOU.
SHAKESPEARE!?
HA! THERE ISN'T ANY WAY THE BOY COULD BE READING THIS.
STILL A BOOK, MR. BEAU. THAT BOY GONNA BE TROUBLE. HE NEEDS TO BE TAMED WITH THE WHIP LIKE I DONE TO HIS PAPPY.
DADDY, IT'S MY FAULT. SAM WAS PUTTING AWAY MY BOOKS, AND I TOLD HIM TO HURRY OUT. HE CAN'T READ.
I WISH I WAS IN THE LAND OF COTTON!

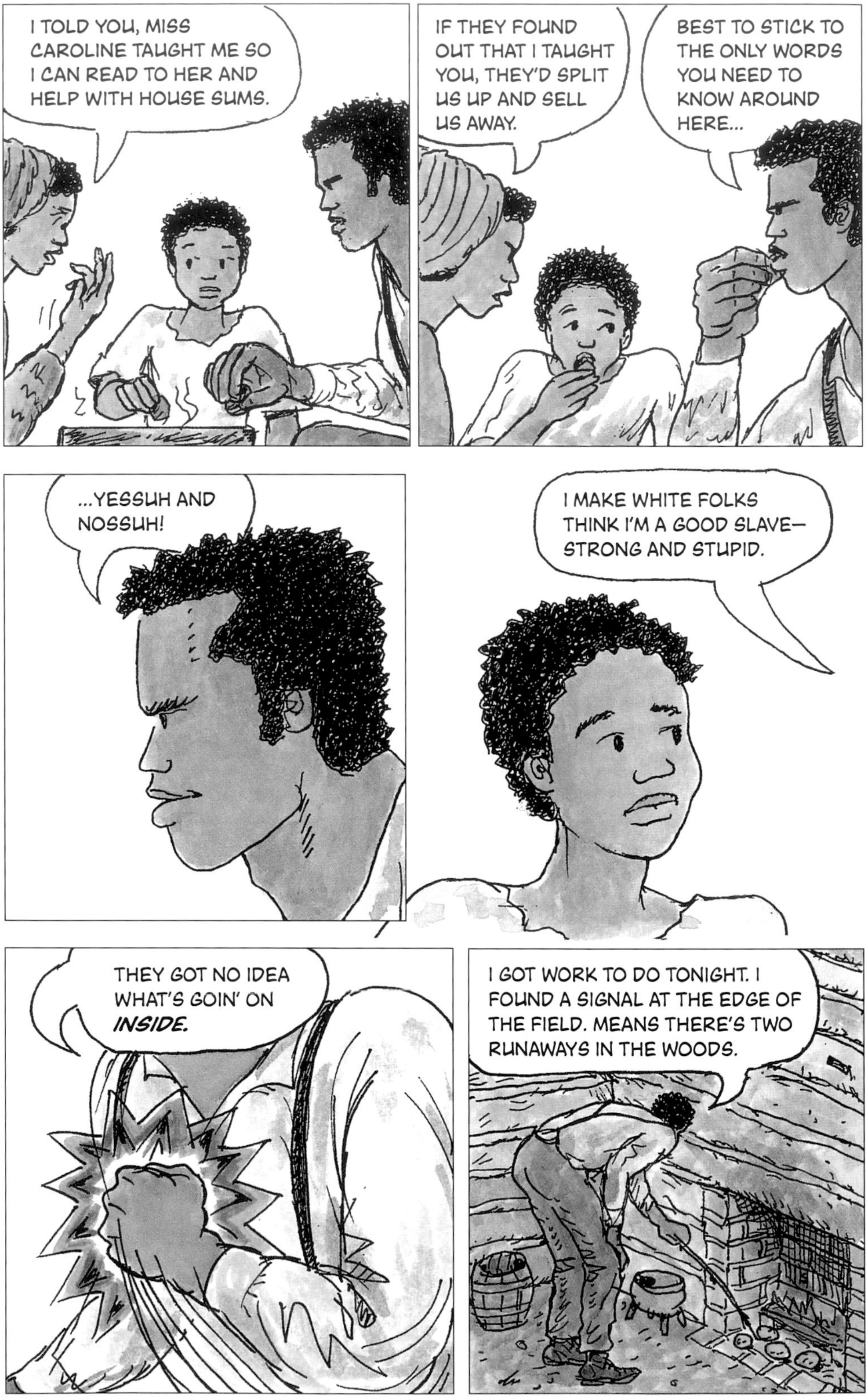
I TOLD YOU, MISS CAROLINE TAUGHT ME SO I CAN READ TO HER AND HELP WITH HOUSE SUMS.
IF THEY FOUND OUT THAT I TAUGHT YOU, THEY'D SPLIT US UP AND SELL US AWAY.
BEST TO STICK TO THE ONLY WORDS YOU NEED TO KNOW AROUND HERE...
...YESSUH AND NOSSUH!
I MAKE WHITE FOLKS THINK I'M A GOOD SLAVE— STRONG AND STUPID.
THEY GOT NO IDEA WHAT'S GOIN' ON *INSIDE.*
I GOT WORK TO DO TONIGHT. I FOUND A SIGNAL AT THE EDGE OF THE FIELD. MEANS THERE'S TWO RUNAWAYS IN THE WOODS.

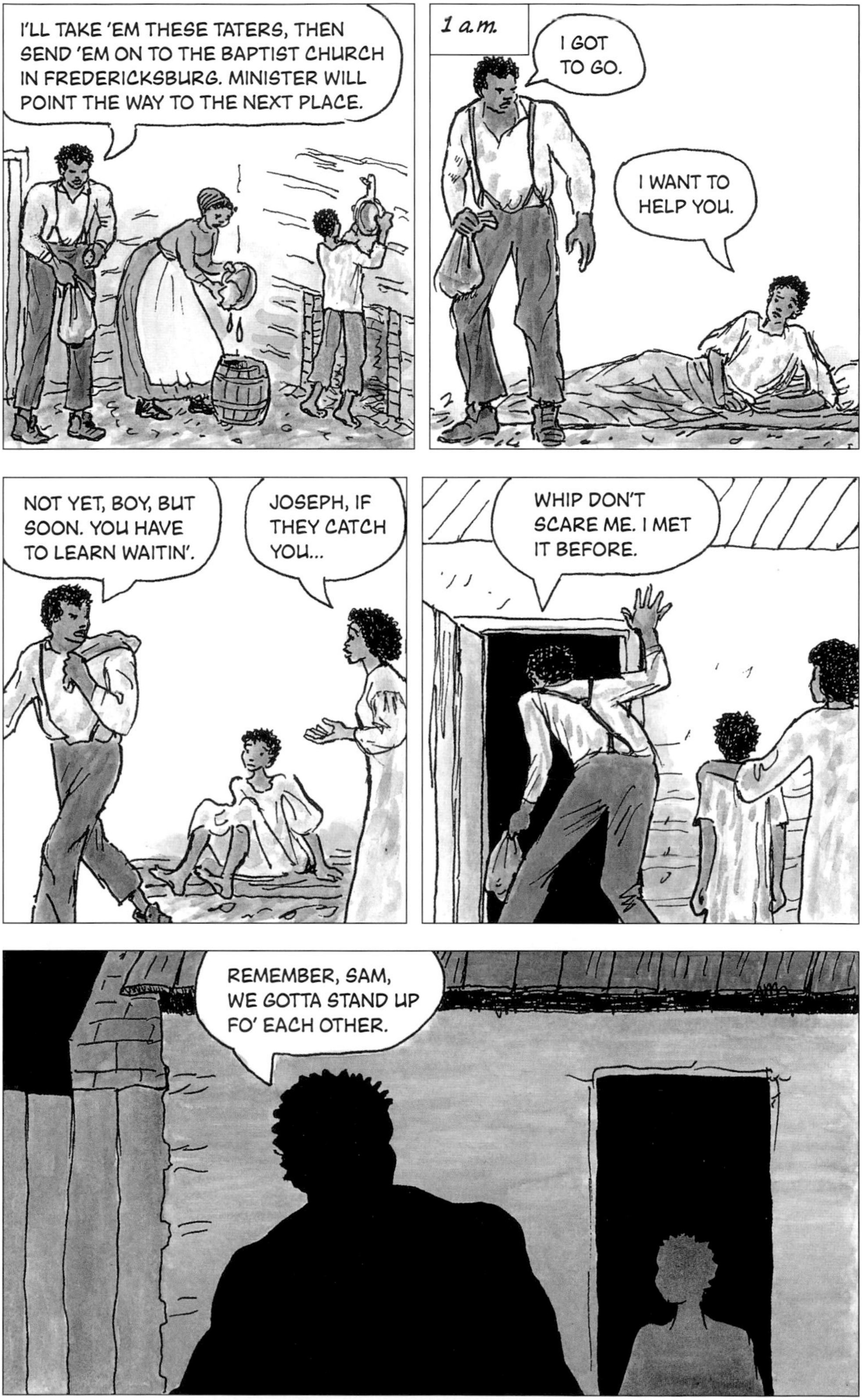
I'LL TAKE 'EM THESE TATERS, THEN SEND 'EM ON TO THE BAPTIST CHURCH IN FREDERICKSBURG. MINISTER WILL POINT THE WAY TO THE NEXT PLACE.
1 a.m.
I GOT TO GO.
I WANT TO HELP YOU.
NOT YET, BOY, BUT SOON. YOU HAVE TO LEARN WAITIN'.
JOSEPH, IF THEY CATCH YOU...
WHIP DON'T SCARE ME. I MET IT BEFORE.
REMEMBER, SAM, WE GOTTA STAND UP FO' EACH OTHER.

CHAPTER 2

As the Confederates continue to succeed on the Virginia battlefields, plantation owners are confident they can hold on to their privileged way of life—and the slaves who make it possible.

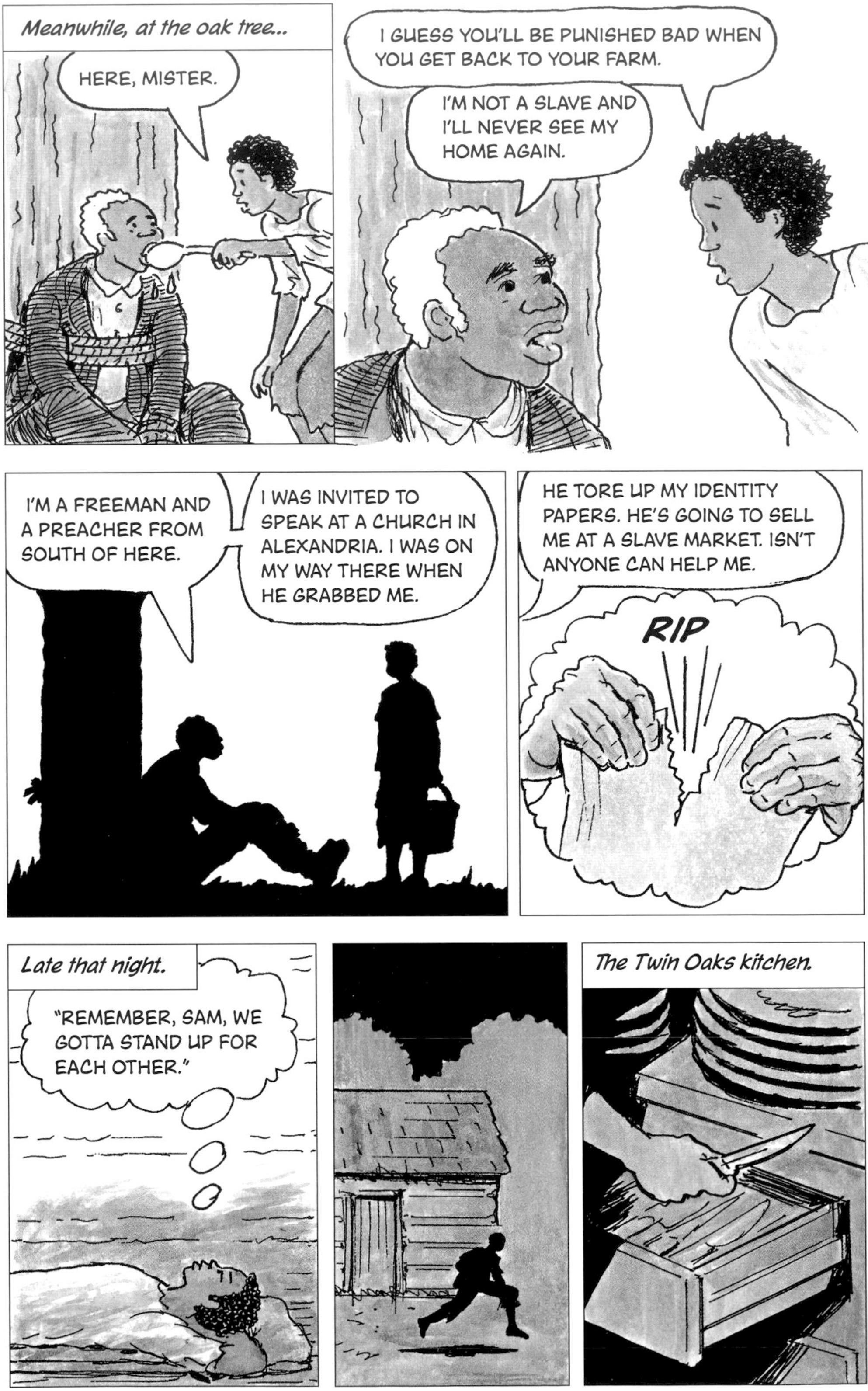

Meanwhile, at the oak tree...
HERE, MISTER.
I GUESS YOU'LL BE PUNISHED BAD WHEN YOU GET BACK TO YOUR FARM.
I'M NOT A SLAVE AND I'LL NEVER SEE MY HOME AGAIN.
I'M A FREEMAN AND A PREACHER FROM SOUTH OF HERE.
I WAS INVITED TO SPEAK AT A CHURCH IN ALEXANDRIA. I WAS ON MY WAY THERE WHEN HE GRABBED ME.
HE TORE UP MY IDENTITY PAPERS. HE'S GOING TO SELL ME AT A SLAVE MARKET. ISN'T ANYONE CAN HELP ME.
RIP
Late that night.
"REMEMBER, SAM, WE GOTTA STAND UP FOR EACH OTHER."
The Twin Oaks kitchen.

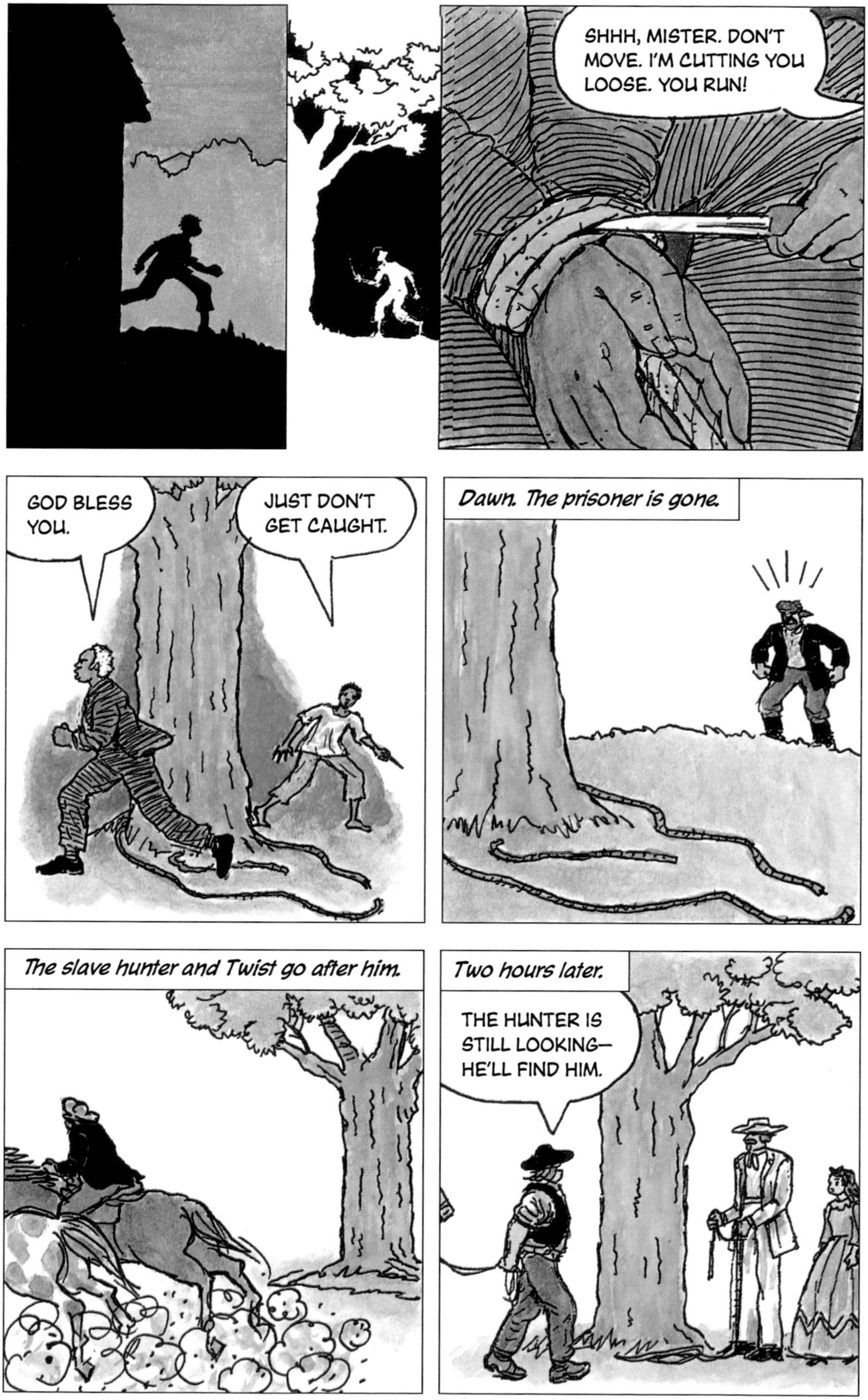
SHHH, MISTER. DON'T MOVE. I'M CUTTING YOU LOOSE. YOU RUN!
GOD BLESS YOU.
JUST DON'T GET CAUGHT.
Dawn. The prisoner is gone.
The slave hunter and Twist go after him.
Two hours later.
THE HUNTER IS STILL LOOKING— HE'LL FIND HIM.

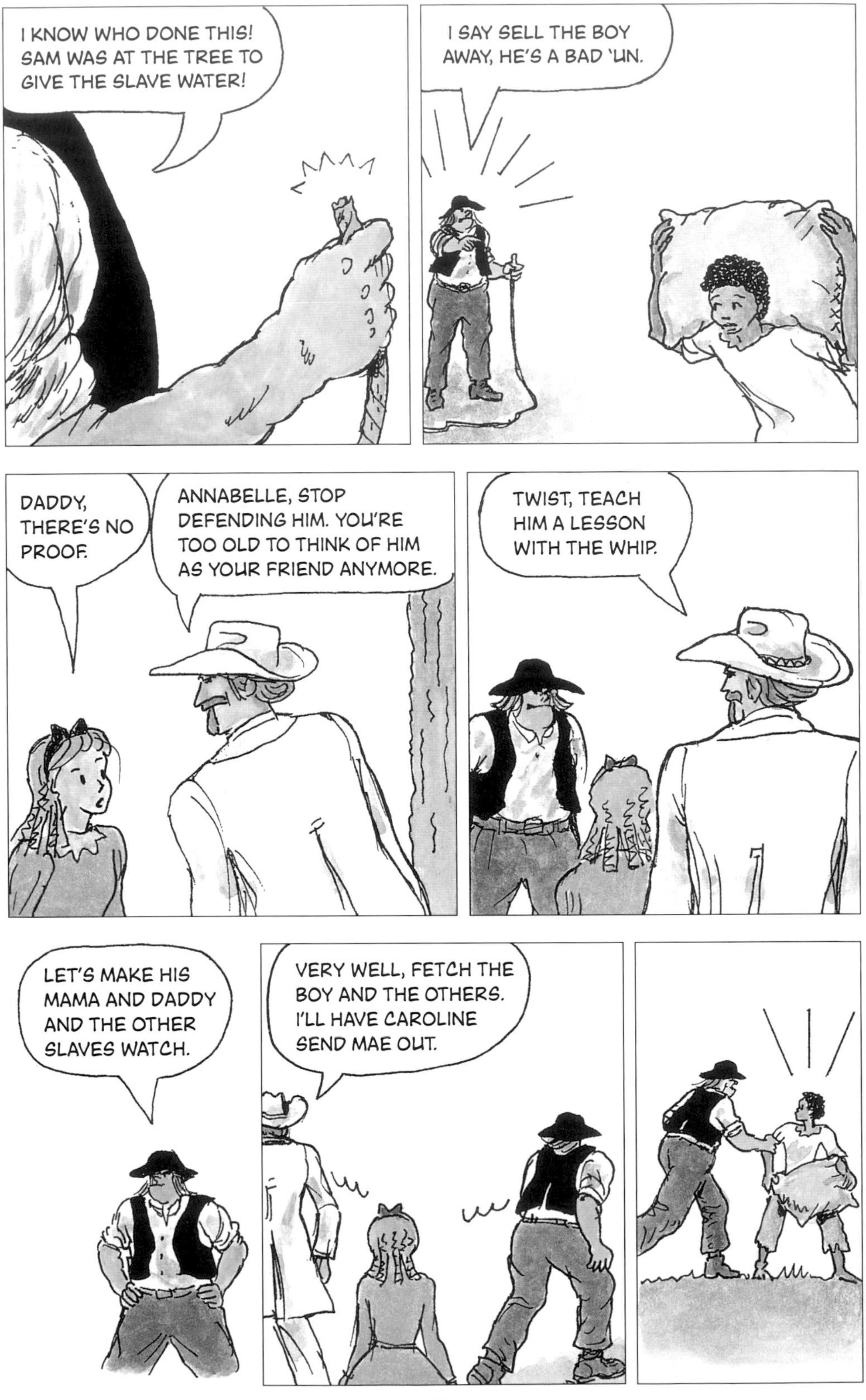
I KNOW WHO DONE THIS! SAM WAS AT THE TREE TO GIVE THE SLAVE WATER!
I SAY SELL THE BOY AWAY, HE'S A BAD 'UN.
DADDY, THERE'S NO PROOF.
ANNABELLE, STOP DEFENDING HIM. YOU'RE TOO OLD TO THINK OF HIM AS YOUR FRIEND ANYMORE.
TWIST, TEACH HIM A LESSON WITH THE WHIP.
LET'S MAKE HIS MAMA AND DADDY AND THE OTHER SLAVES WATCH.
VERY WELL, FETCH THE BOY AND THE OTHERS. I'LL HAVE CAROLINE SEND MAE OUT.

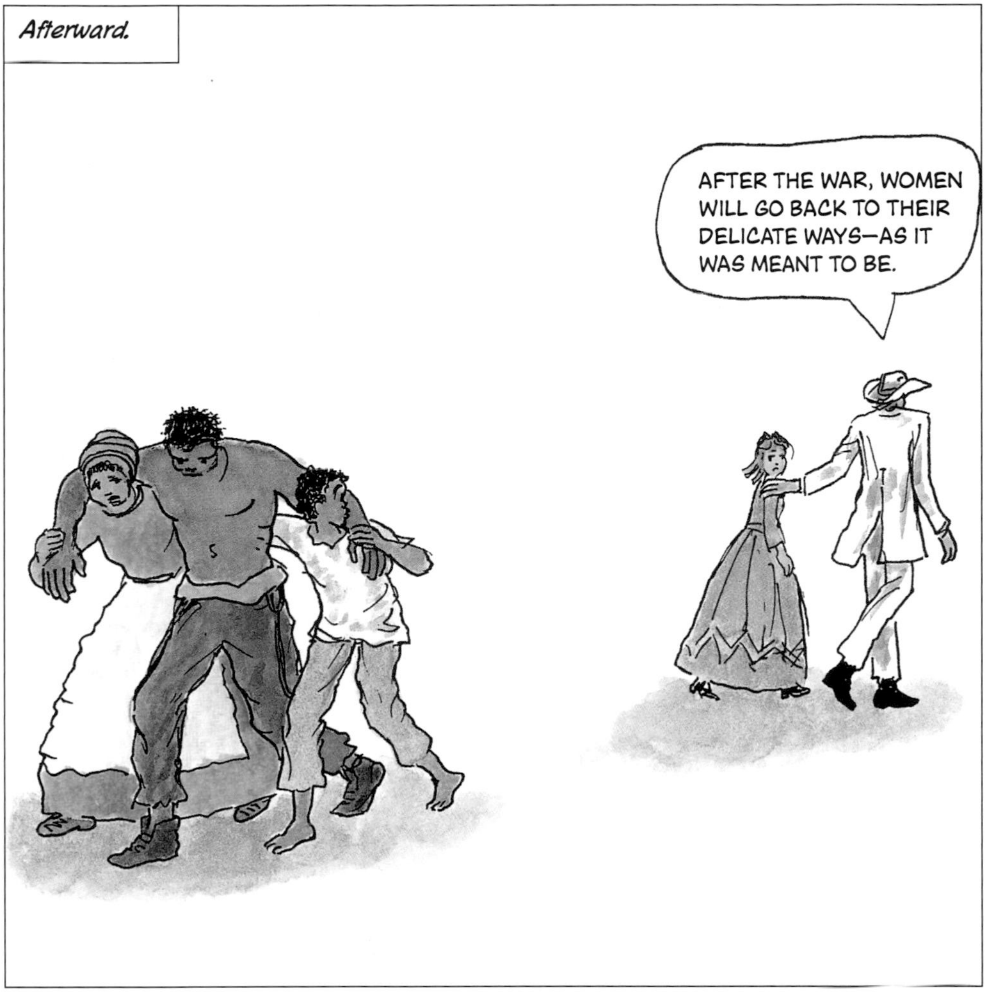
Afterward.
AFTER THE WAR, WOMEN WILL GO BACK TO THEIR DELICATE WAYS—AS IT WAS MEANT TO BE.

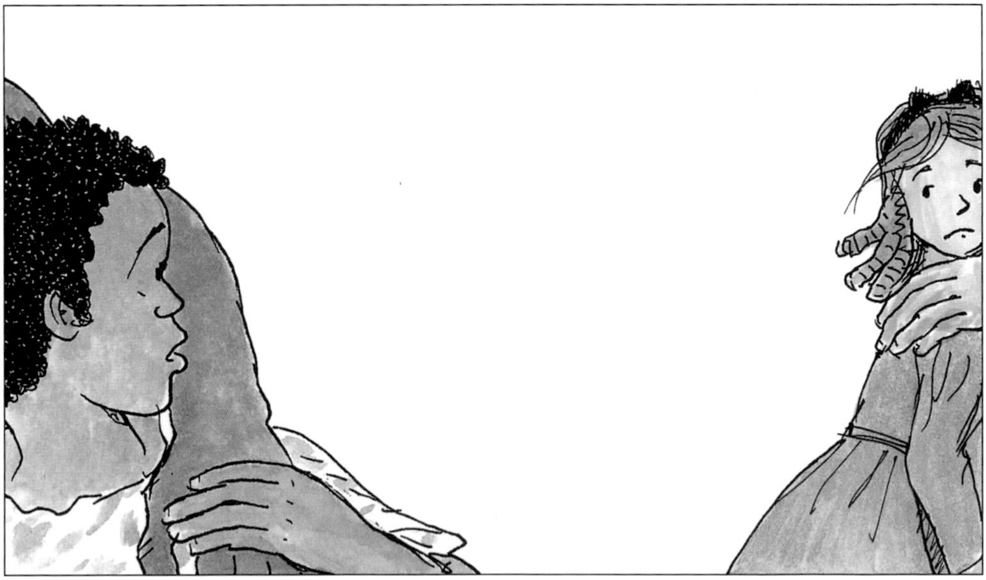

CHAPTER 3

On July 17, 1862, Lincoln signs the Second Confiscation Act. It says that slaves from Confederate states who reach Union lines will be considered captives of war and "free of their servitude."

23

25

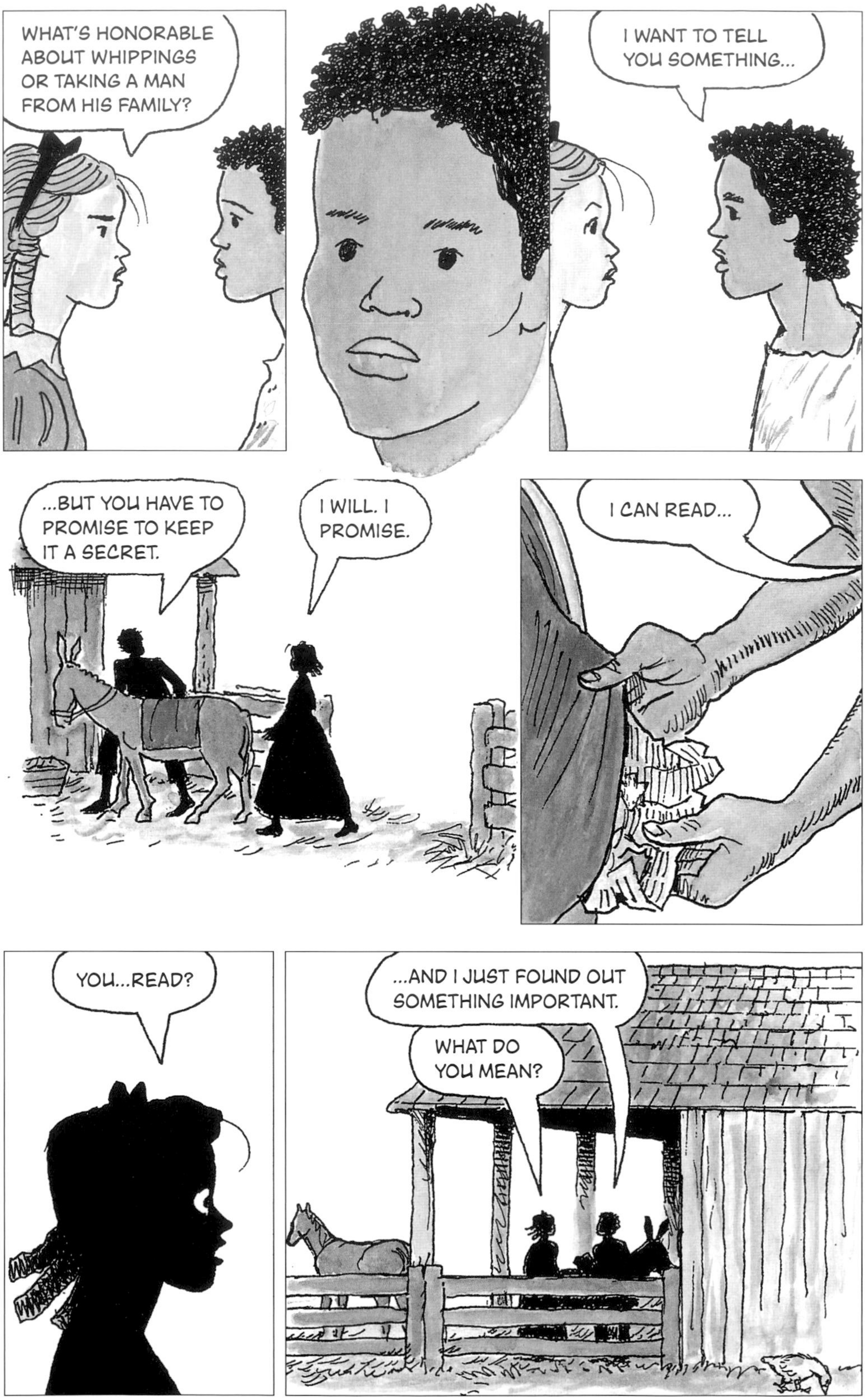
WHAT'S HONORABLE ABOUT WHIPPINGS OR TAKING A MAN FROM HIS FAMILY?
I WANT TO TELL YOU SOMETHING...
...BUT YOU HAVE TO PROMISE TO KEEP IT A SECRET.
I WILL. I PROMISE.
I CAN READ...
YOU...READ?
...AND I JUST FOUND OUT SOMETHING IMPORTANT.
WHAT DO YOU MEAN?

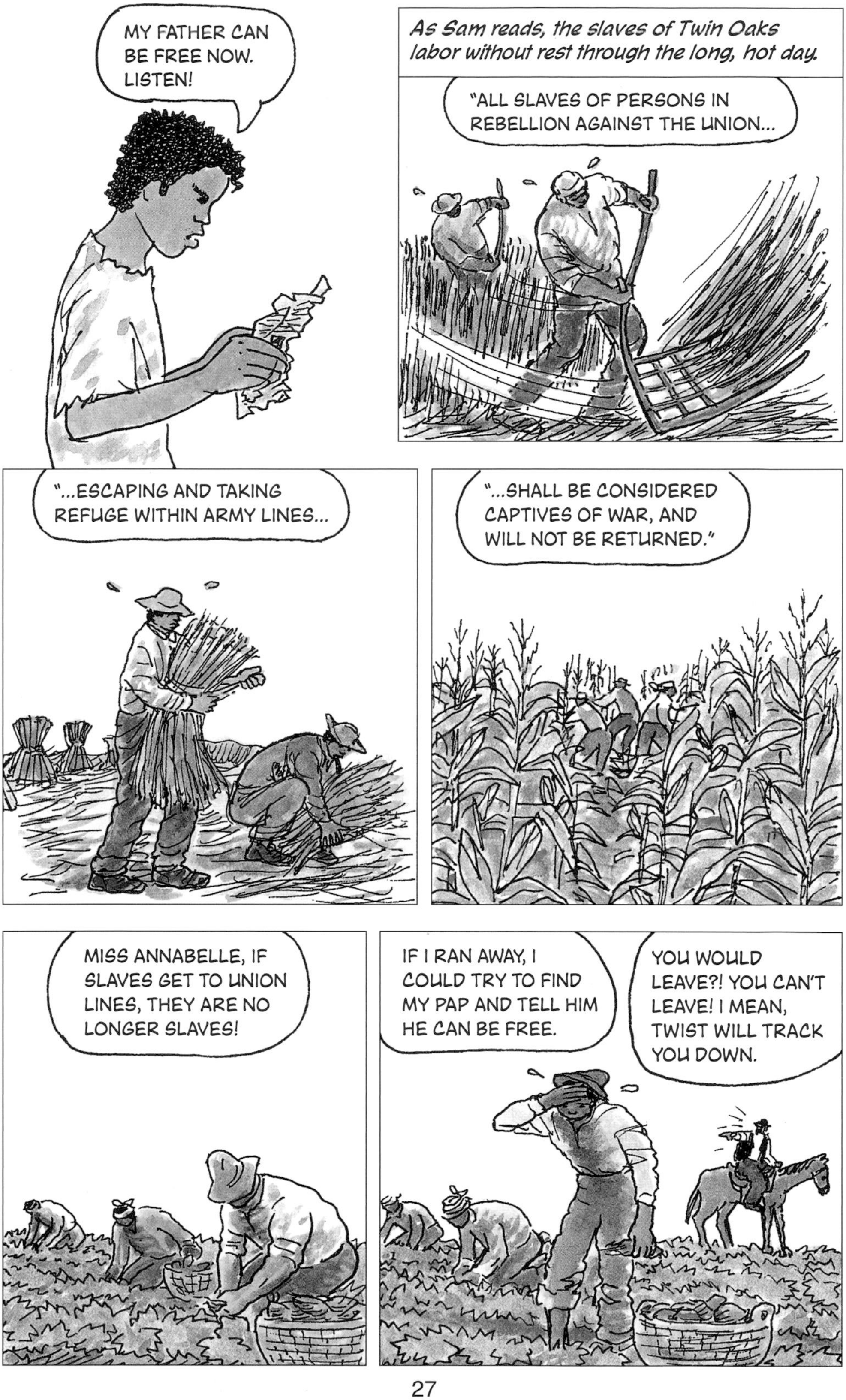
MY FATHER CAN BE FREE NOW. LISTEN!
As Sam reads, the slaves of Twin Oaks labor without rest through the long, hot day.
"ALL SLAVES OF PERSONS IN REBELLION AGAINST THE UNION...
"...ESCAPING AND TAKING REFUGE WITHIN ARMY LINES...
"...SHALL BE CONSIDERED CAPTIVES OF WAR, AND WILL NOT BE RETURNED."
MISS ANNABELLE, IF SLAVES GET TO UNION LINES, THEY ARE NO LONGER SLAVES!
IF I RAN AWAY, I COULD TRY TO FIND MY PAP AND TELL HIM HE CAN BE FREE.
YOU WOULD LEAVE?! YOU CAN'T LEAVE! I MEAN, TWIST WILL TRACK YOU DOWN.

28

29

CHAPTER 4

A confident Lee attempts to move the fighting north but is stopped on September 17, 1862, at Antietam Creek, Maryland. The battle is known as Antietam by the North, Sharpsburg by the South. There's no clear-cut victory in what is called the bloodiest one-day battle in U.S. history. Lee retreats to Virginia.

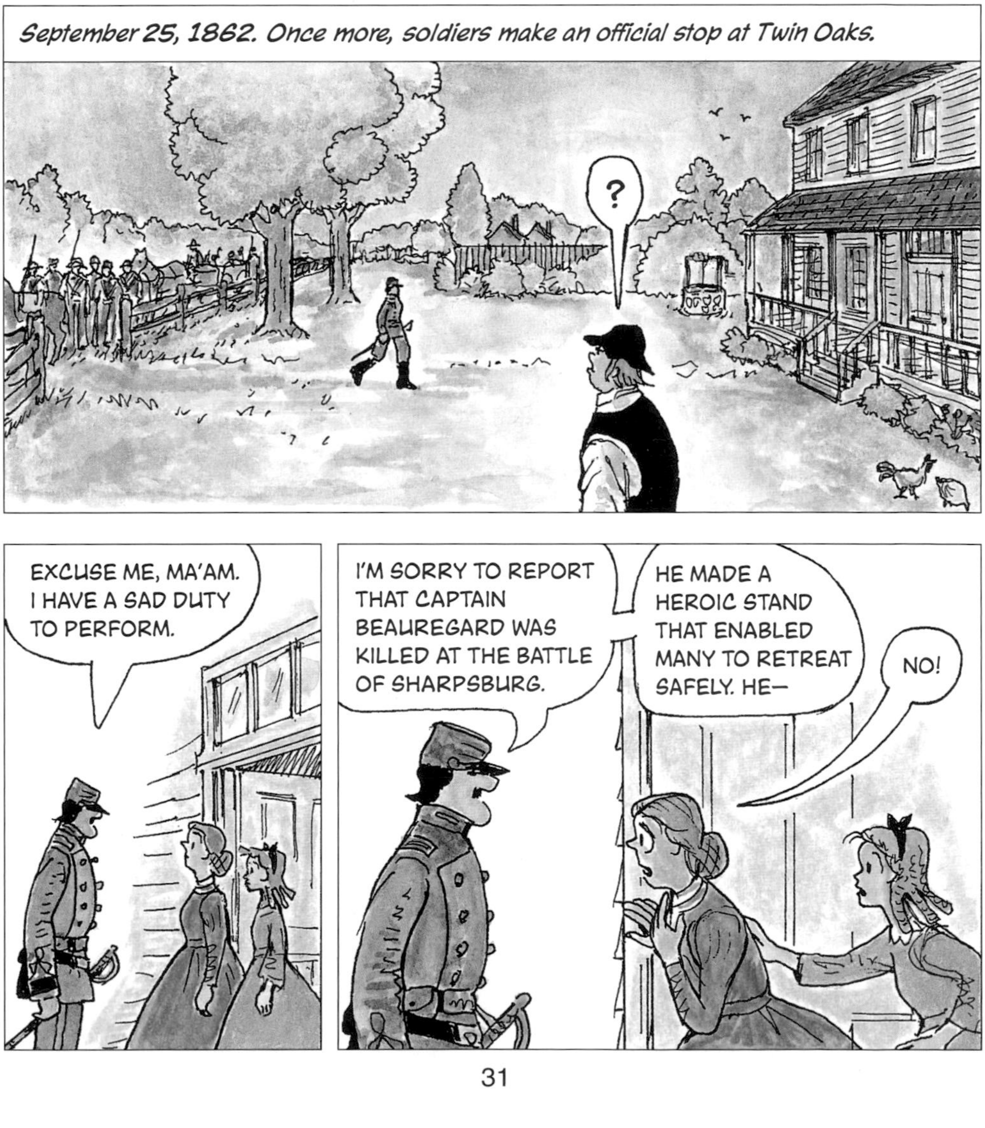

September 25, 1862. Once more, soldiers make an official stop at Twin Oaks.
?
EXCUSE ME, MA'AM. I HAVE A SAD DUTY TO PERFORM.
I'M SORRY TO REPORT THAT CAPTAIN BEAUREGARD WAS KILLED AT THE BATTLE OF SHARPSBURG.
HE MADE A HEROIC STAND THAT ENABLED MANY TO RETREAT SAFELY. HE—
NO!

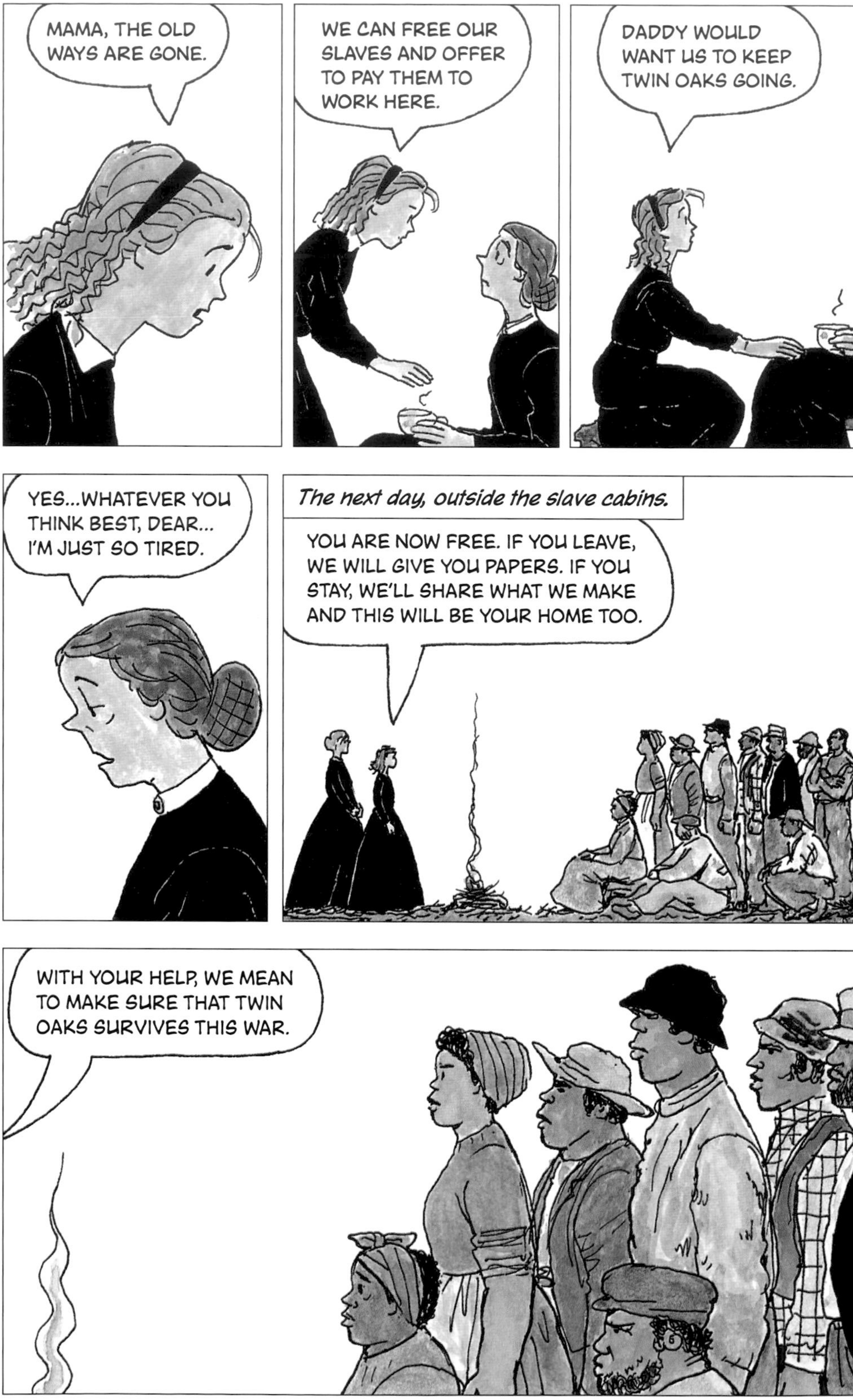

MAMA, THE OLD WAYS ARE GONE.
WE CAN FREE OUR SLAVES AND OFFER TO PAY THEM TO WORK HERE.
DADDY WOULD WANT US TO KEEP TWIN OAKS GOING.
YES...WHATEVER YOU THINK BEST, DEAR... I'M JUST SO TIRED.
The next day, outside the slave cabins.
YOU ARE NOW FREE. IF YOU LEAVE, WE WILL GIVE YOU PAPERS. IF YOU STAY, WE'LL SHARE WHAT WE MAKE AND THIS WILL BE YOUR HOME TOO.
WITH YOUR HELP, WE MEAN TO MAKE SURE THAT TWIN OAKS SURVIVES THIS WAR.

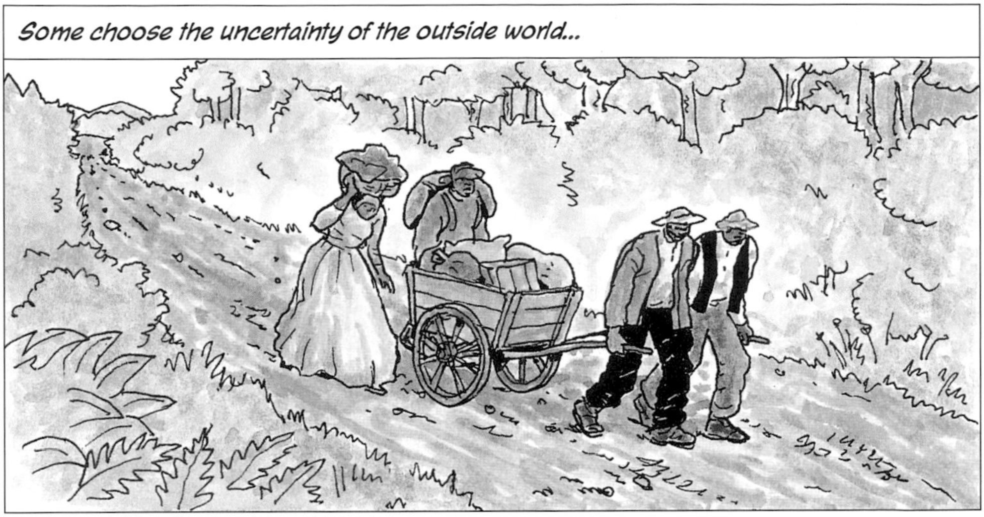
Some choose the uncertainty of the outside world...

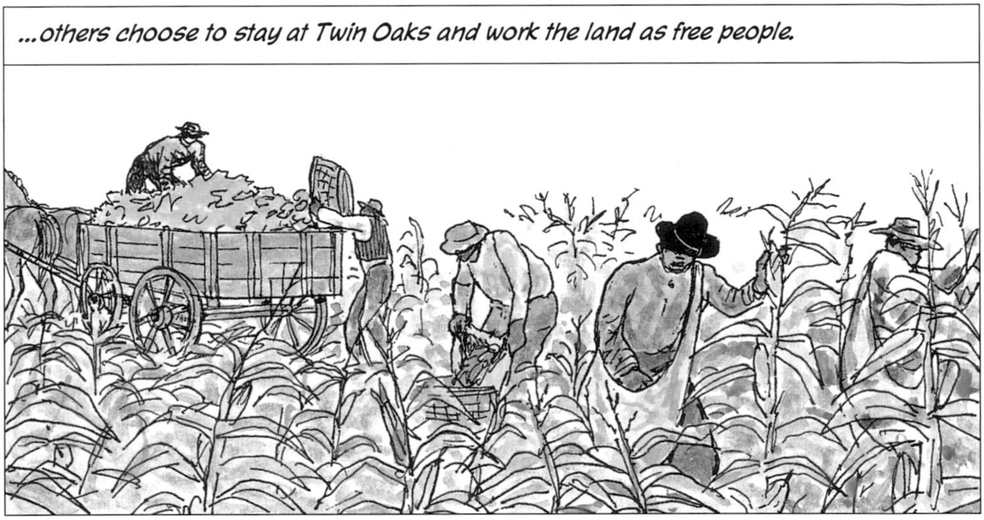
...others choose to stay at Twin Oaks and work the land as free people.

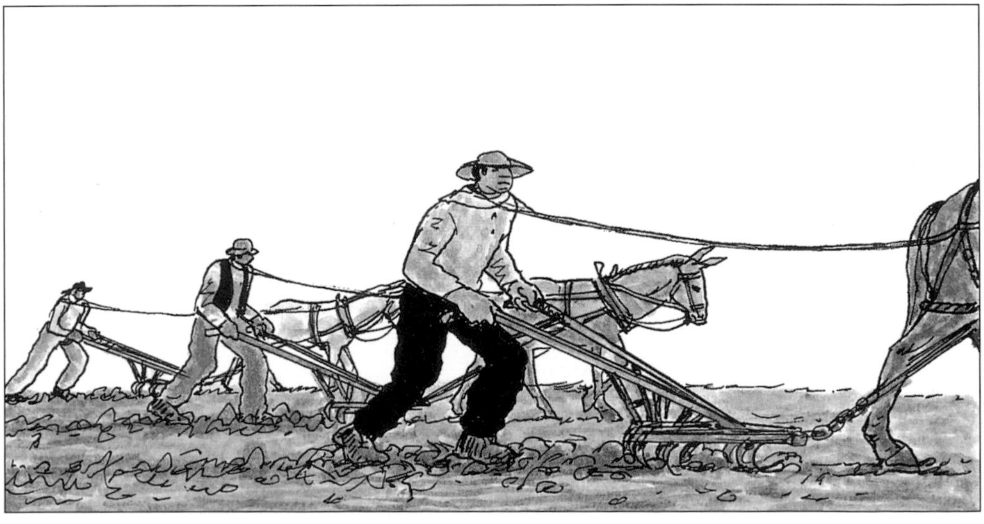

CHAPTER 5

Runaway slaves, seeking refuge, begin to overwhelm Union Army outposts. The government and aid groups step in to provide assistance to men, women, and children who have never known anything but bondage.

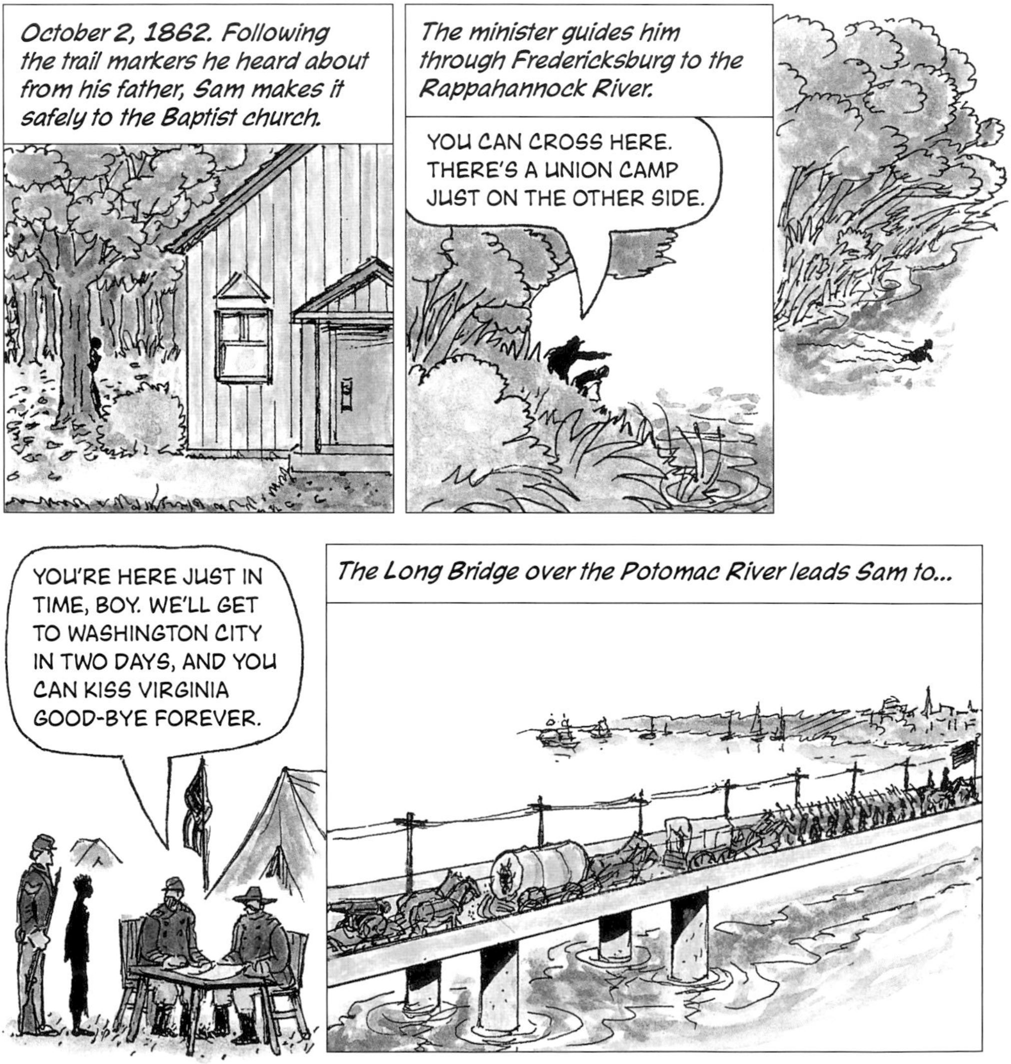

October 2, 1862. Following the trail markers he heard about from his father, Sam makes it safely to the Baptist church.
The minister guides him through Fredericksburg to the Rappahannock River.
YOU CAN CROSS HERE. THERE'S A UNION CAMP JUST ON THE OTHER SIDE.
YOU'RE HERE JUST IN TIME, BOY. WE'LL GET TO WASHINGTON CITY IN TWO DAYS, AND YOU CAN KISS VIRGINIA GOOD-BYE FOREVER.
The Long Bridge over the Potomac River leads Sam to...

43

46

47

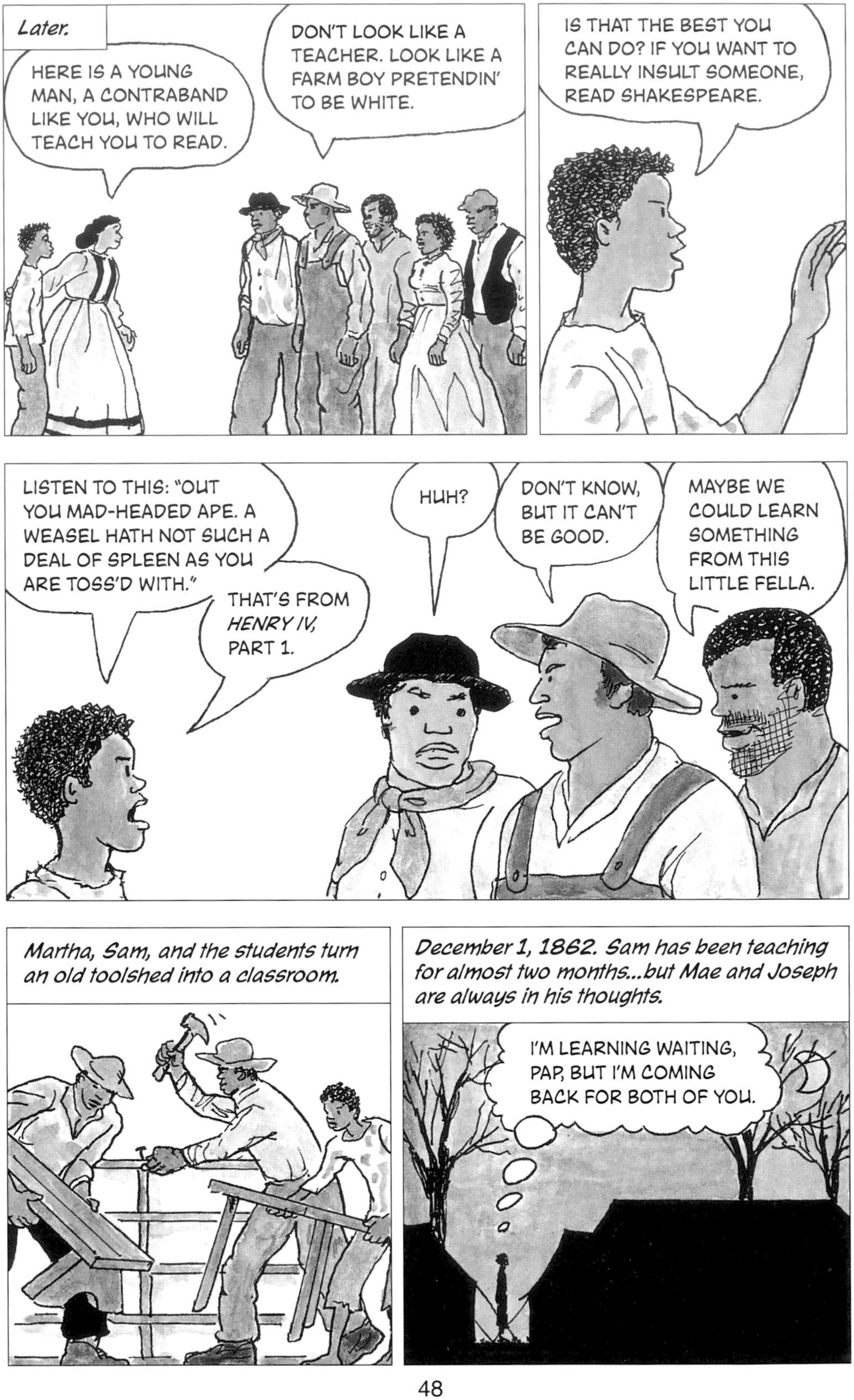

Later.
HERE IS A YOUNG MAN, A CONTRABAND LIKE YOU, WHO WILL TEACH YOU TO READ.
DON'T LOOK LIKE A TEACHER. LOOK LIKE A FARM BOY PRETENDIN' TO BE WHITE.
IS THAT THE BEST YOU CAN DO? IF YOU WANT TO REALLY INSULT SOMEONE, READ SHAKESPEARE.
LISTEN TO THIS: "OUT YOU MAD-HEADED APE. A WEASEL HATH NOT SUCH A DEAL OF SPLEEN AS YOU ARE TOSS'D WITH."
THAT'S FROM *HENRY IV*, PART 1.
HUH?
DON'T KNOW, BUT IT CAN'T BE GOOD.
MAYBE WE COULD LEARN SOMETHING FROM THIS LITTLE FELLA.
Martha, Sam, and the students turn an old toolshed into a classroom.
December 1, 1862. Sam has been teaching for almost two months...but Mae and Joseph are always in his thoughts.
I'M LEARNING WAITING, PAP, BUT I'M COMING BACK FOR BOTH OF YOU.

51

CHAPTER 6

The war is draining Southern farms and towns of their able-bodied men. At home, folks must try to survive in a war-battered countryside. It's a situation ready-made for homegrown thieves.

December 1862. Back in Virginia, Annabelle, Caroline, and the former slaves work together, producing enough to feed themselves and to sell and barter at local markets.

WE'VE GOT GOOD-LOOKING SWEET POTATOES AND DELICIOUS PICKLED PEACHES.

Annabelle takes on new roles, from decision maker to field hand.

53

As Twin Oaks's reputation spreads, a stream of Lee's men, suffering from disease brought on by cold and unsanitary conditions, begins to arrive. No one is turned away.

CHAPTER 7

On December 12, 1862, the Union Army attacks across the Rappahannock River at Fredericksburg. The well-protected Confederate Army kills thousands and drives the Union Army back across the river. President Lincoln loses all hope that the war can be resolved quickly.

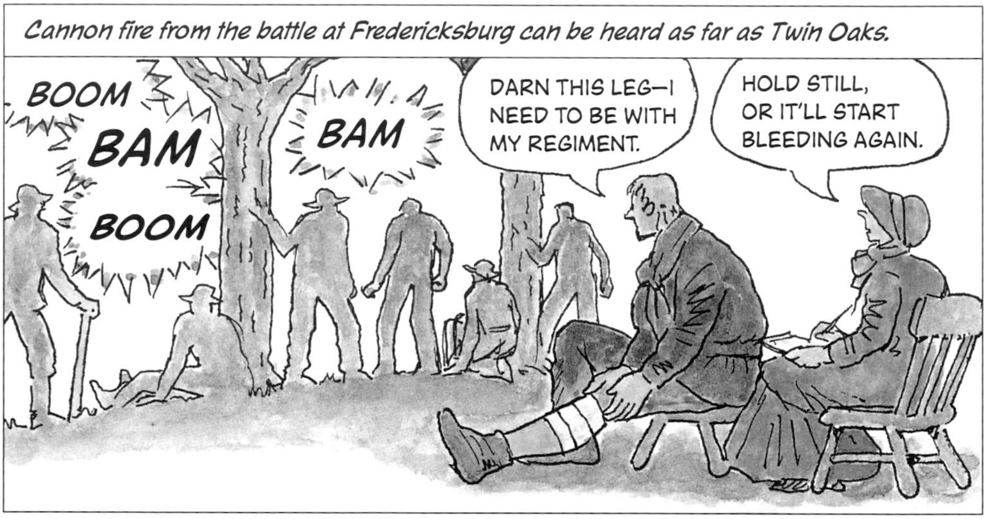
Cannon fire from the battle at Fredericksburg can be heard as far as Twin Oaks.
BOOM
BAM
BOOM
BAM
DARN THIS LEG—I NEED TO BE WITH MY REGIMENT.
HOLD STILL, OR IT'LL START BLEEDING AGAIN.

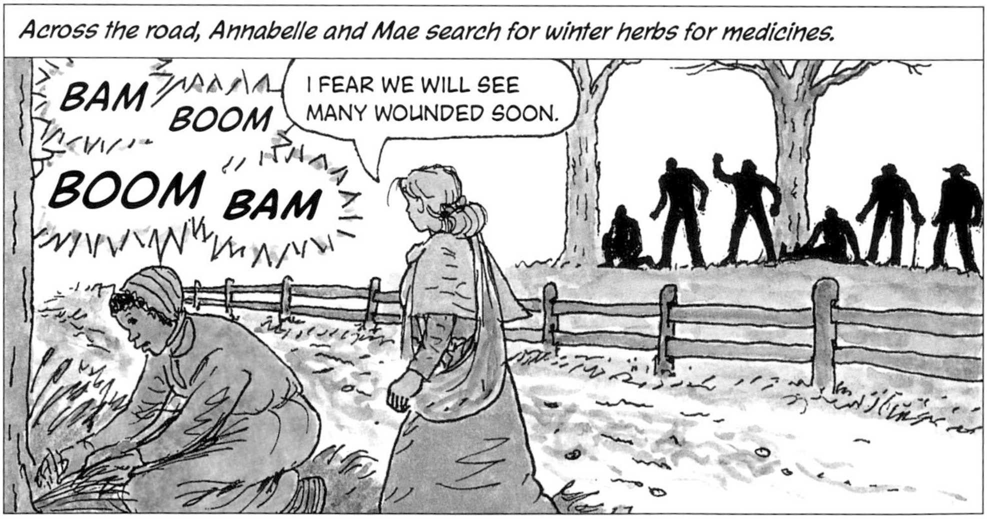
Across the road, Annabelle and Mae search for winter herbs for medicines.
BAM
BOOM
BOOM
BAM
I FEAR WE WILL SEE MANY WOUNDED SOON.

59

61

January 10, 1863. On a tour of army camps, President Lincoln visits Camp Barker.

65

66

67

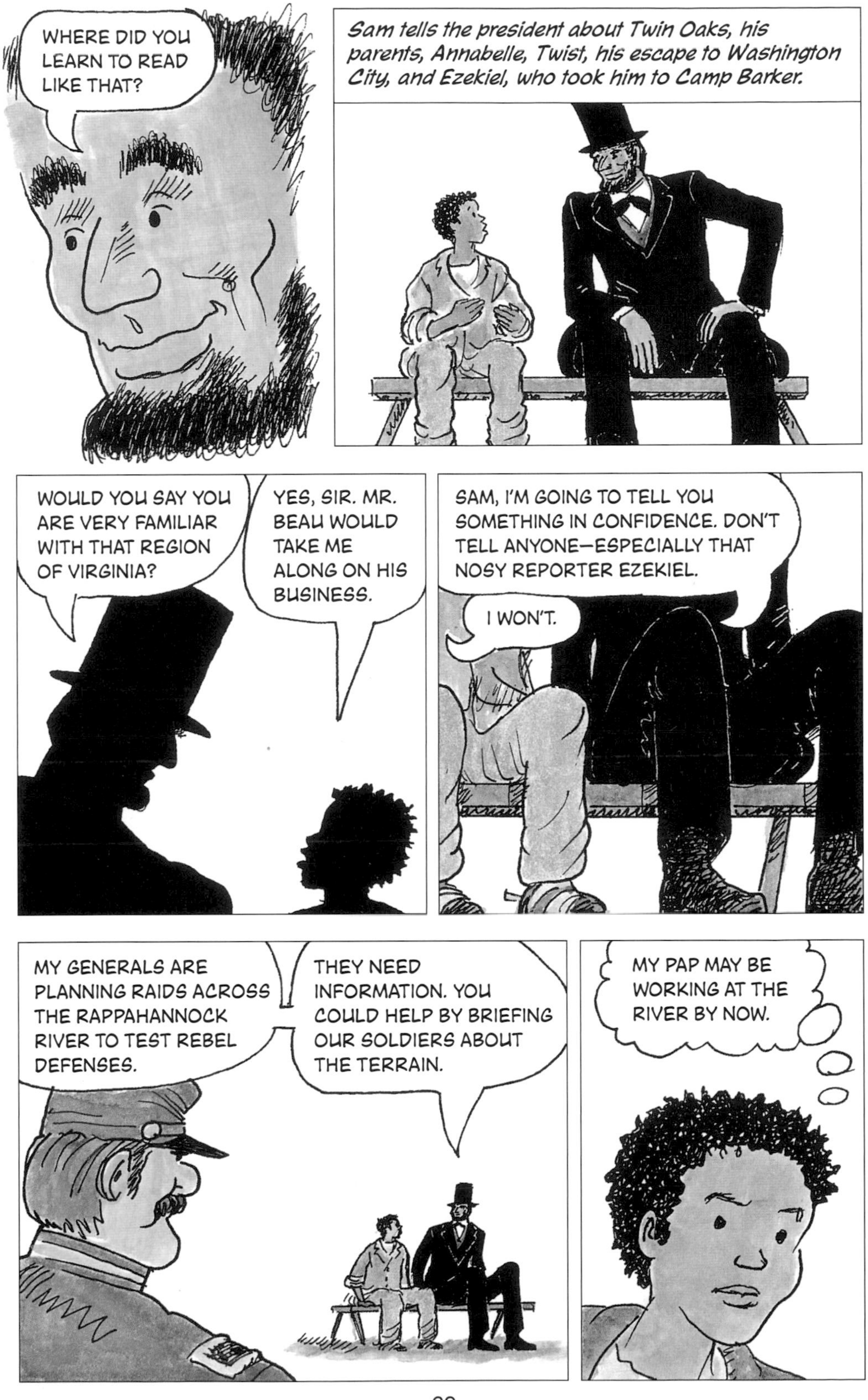
WHERE DID YOU LEARN TO READ LIKE THAT?
Sam tells the president about Twin Oaks, his parents, Annabelle, Twist, his escape to Washington City, and Ezekiel, who took him to Camp Barker.
WOULD YOU SAY YOU ARE VERY FAMILIAR WITH THAT REGION OF VIRGINIA?
YES, SIR. MR. BEAU WOULD TAKE ME ALONG ON HIS BUSINESS.
SAM, I'M GOING TO TELL YOU SOMETHING IN CONFIDENCE. DON'T TELL ANYONE—ESPECIALLY THAT NOSY REPORTER EZEKIEL.
I WON'T.
MY GENERALS ARE PLANNING RAIDS ACROSS THE RAPPAHANNOCK RIVER TO TEST REBEL DEFENSES.
THEY NEED INFORMATION. YOU COULD HELP BY BRIEFING OUR SOLDIERS ABOUT THE TERRAIN.
MY PAP MAY BE WORKING AT THE RIVER BY NOW.

CHAPTER 8

Early in 1863, the North prepares for a major spring offensive in Virginia. At the same time, both sides wonder if and how the Emancipation Proclamation will affect the course of the war.

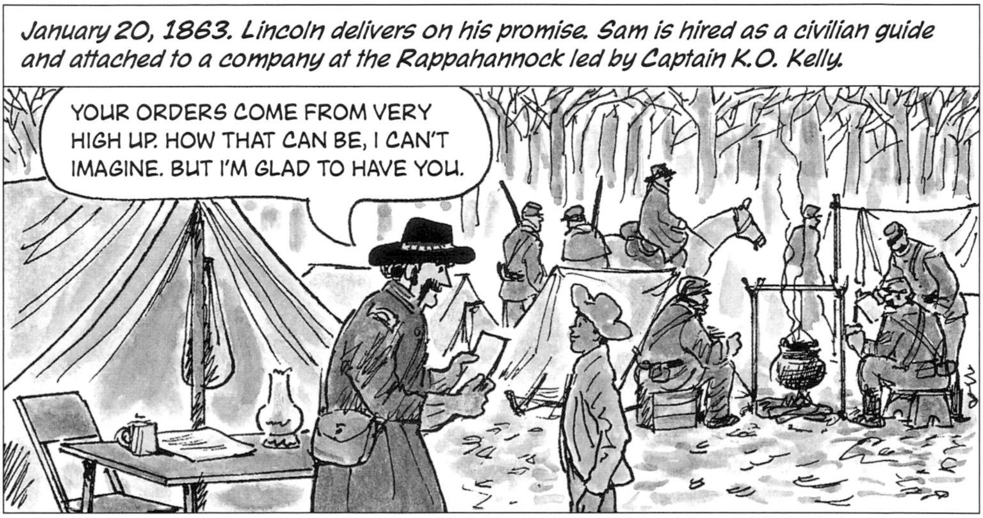
January 20, 1863. Lincoln delivers on his promise. Sam is hired as a civilian guide and attached to a company at the Rappahannock led by Captain K.O. Kelly.
YOUR ORDERS COME FROM VERY HIGH UP. HOW THAT CAN BE, I CAN'T IMAGINE. BUT I'M GLAD TO HAVE YOU.

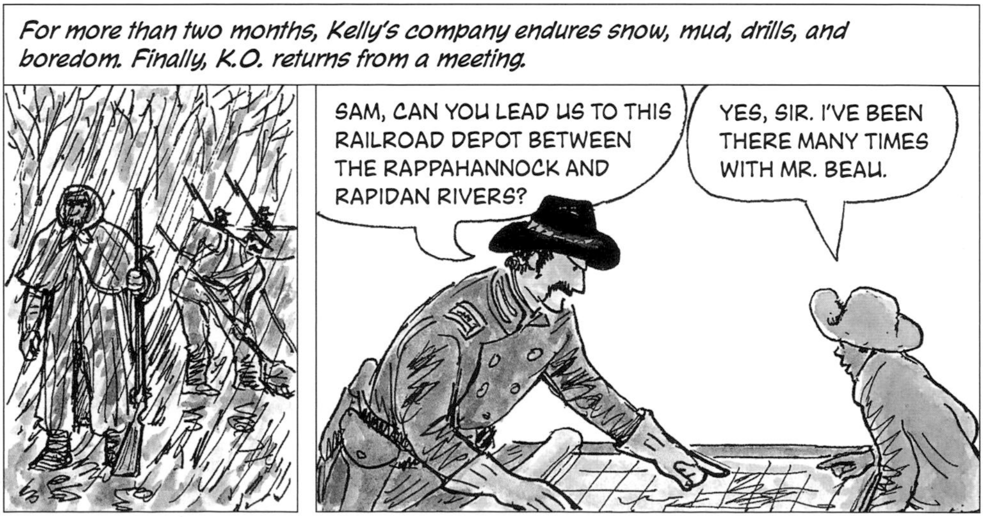
For more than two months, Kelly's company endures snow, mud, drills, and boredom. Finally, K.O. returns from a meeting.
SAM, CAN YOU LEAD US TO THIS RAILROAD DEPOT BETWEEN THE RAPPAHANNOCK AND RAPIDAN RIVERS?
YES, SIR. I'VE BEEN THERE MANY TIMES WITH MR. BEAU.

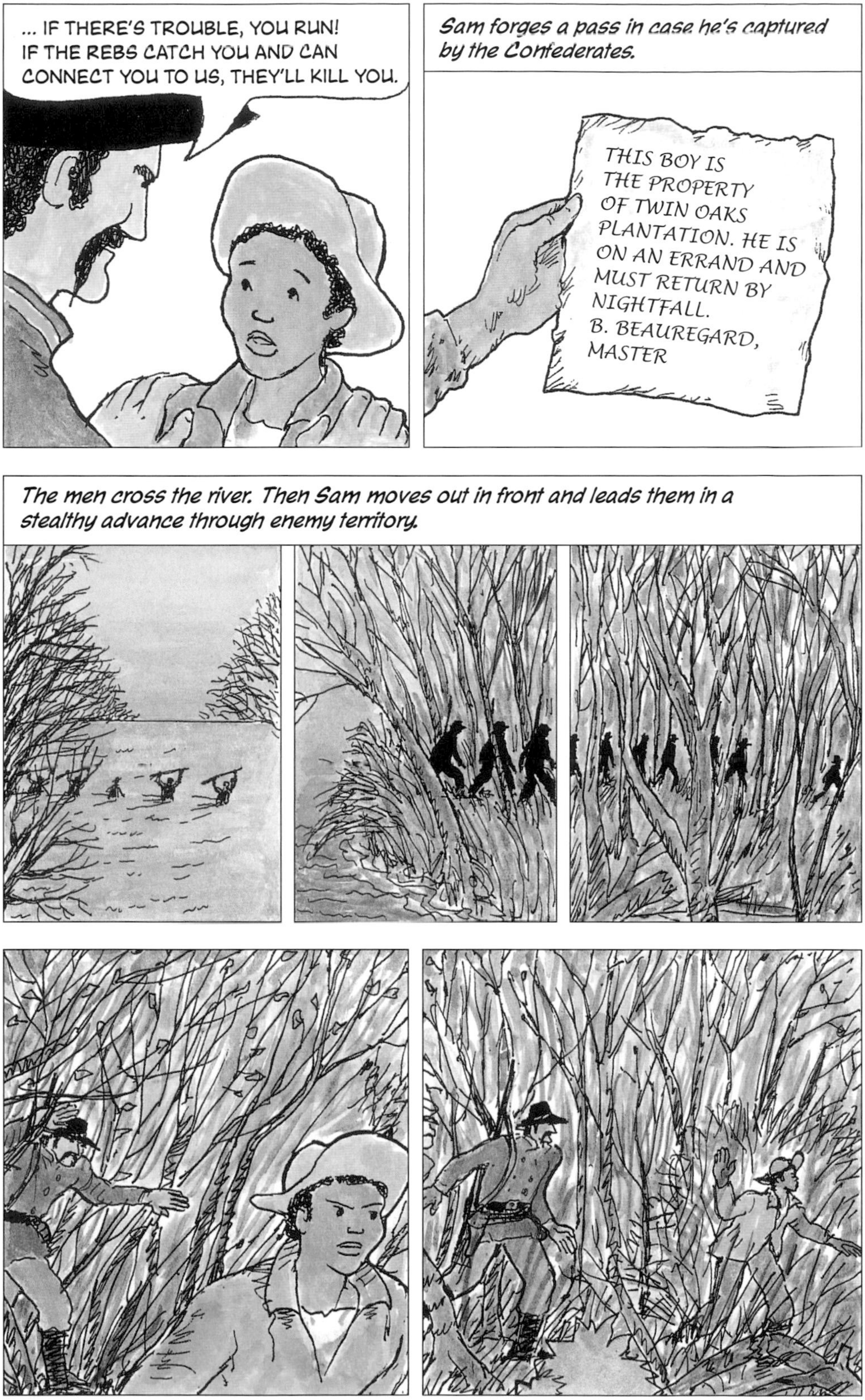
... IF THERE'S TROUBLE, YOU RUN! IF THE REBS CATCH YOU AND CAN CONNECT YOU TO US, THEY'LL KILL YOU.
Sam forges a pass in case he's captured by the Confederates.
THIS BOY IS THE PROPERTY OF TWIN OAKS PLANTATION. HE IS ON AN ERRAND AND MUST RETURN BY NIGHTFALL. B. BEAUREGARD, MASTER
The men cross the river. Then Sam moves out in front and leads them in a stealthy advance through enemy territory.

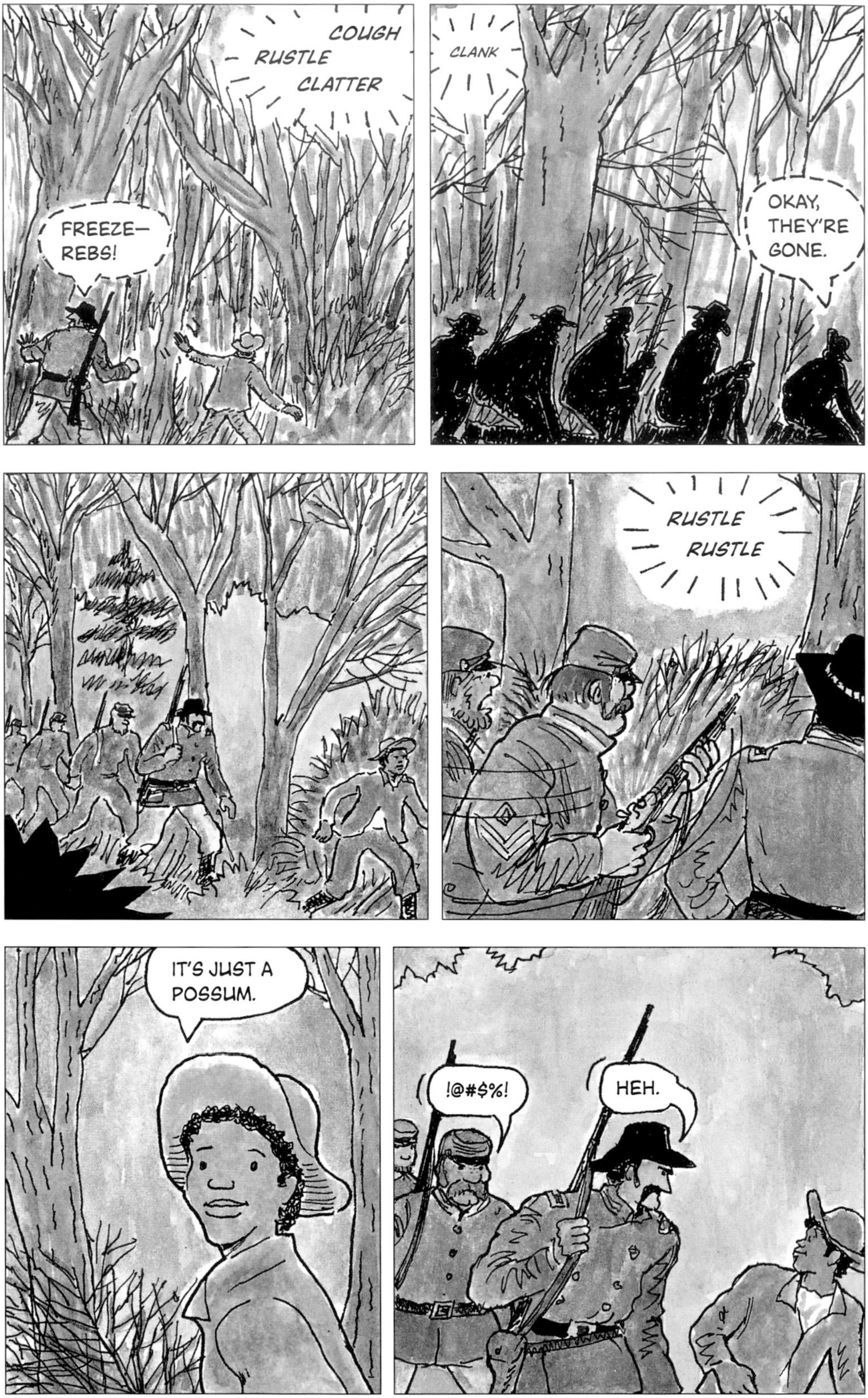
COUGH
RUSTLE
CLATTER
FREEZE—
REBS!
CLANK
OKAY, THEY'RE GONE.
RUSTLE
RUSTLE
IT'S JUST A POSSUM.
!@#$%!
HEH.

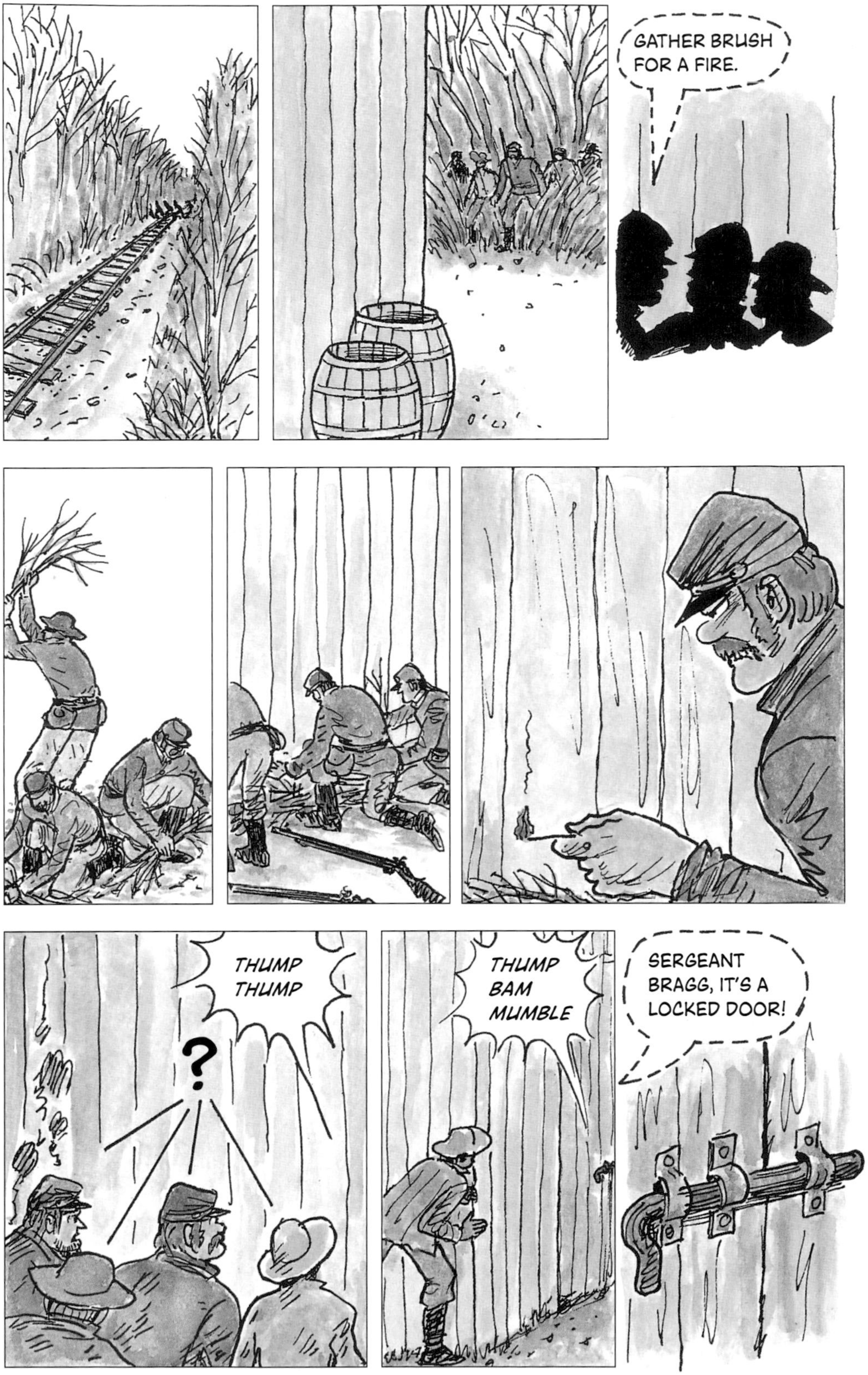
GATHER BRUSH FOR A FIRE.
THUMP THUMP
?
THUMP BAM MUMBLE
SERGEANT BRAGG, IT'S A LOCKED DOOR!

78

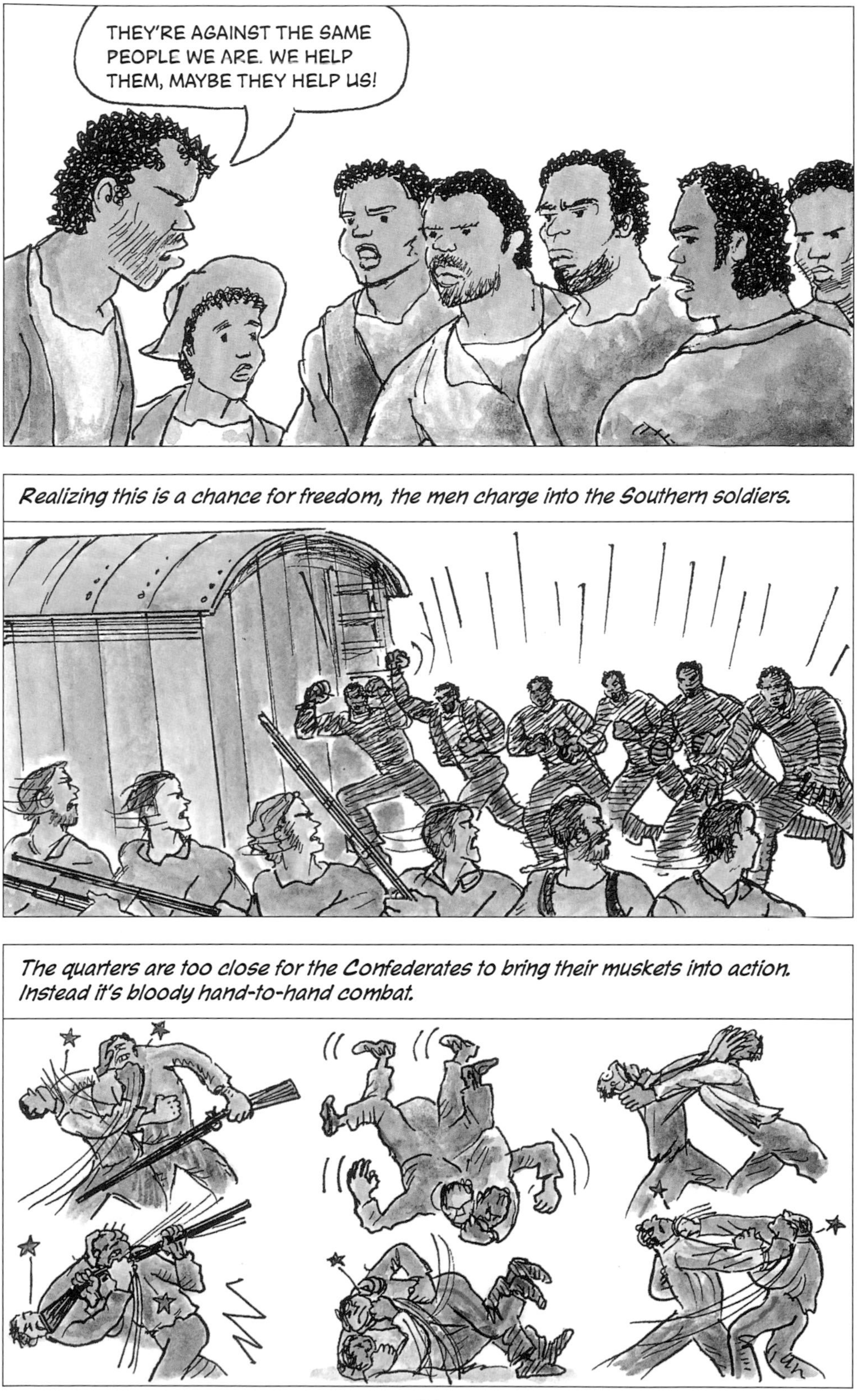
THEY'RE AGAINST THE SAME PEOPLE WE ARE. WE HELP THEM, MAYBE THEY HELP US!
Realizing this is a chance for freedom, the men charge into the Southern soldiers.
The quarters are too close for the Confederates to bring their muskets into action. Instead it's bloody hand-to-hand combat.

The Confederates are tough, but the freed slaves are relentless in their attack. They beat down their enemy and give Kelly and his men time to regroup.

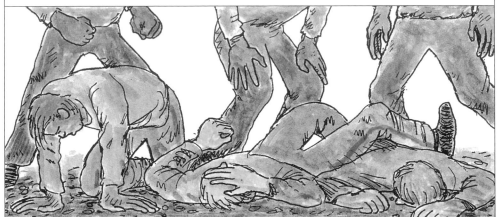

Just then...

BOOM
BOOM BOOM

THERE GOES THE AMMUNITION! THIS IS OUR CHANCE! *SAM, BRING EVERYONE! GET BEHIND US!*

MEN, WITHDRAW IN ORDER! SHOOT ANY REB WHO GOES FOR HIS GUN!

BAM

WHEN WE REACH THE WOODS, *RUN FOR THE RIVER LIKE THE DEVIL HIMSELF IS AFTER YOU!*

RETRIEVE YOUR WEAPONS!

BAM BAM

AGH!

CHAPTER 9

As the Union Army prepares another attack across the Rappahannock against General Lee, Lee's support in the South remains strong. But the old Southern lifestyle will never return.

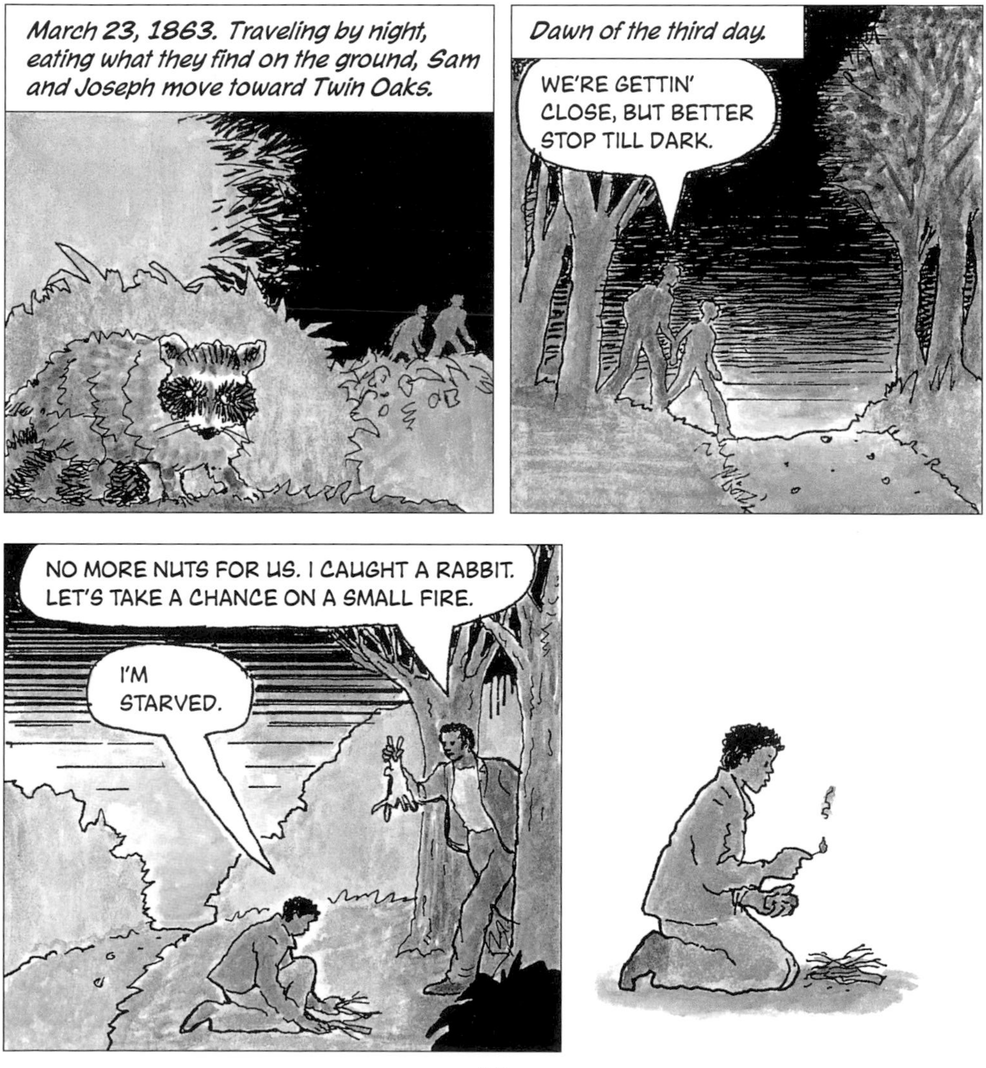
March 23, 1863. Traveling by night, eating what they find on the ground, Sam and Joseph move toward Twin Oaks.
Dawn of the third day.
WE'RE GETTIN' CLOSE, BUT BETTER STOP TILL DARK.
NO MORE NUTS FOR US. I CAUGHT A RABBIT. LET'S TAKE A CHANCE ON A SMALL FIRE.
I'M STARVED.

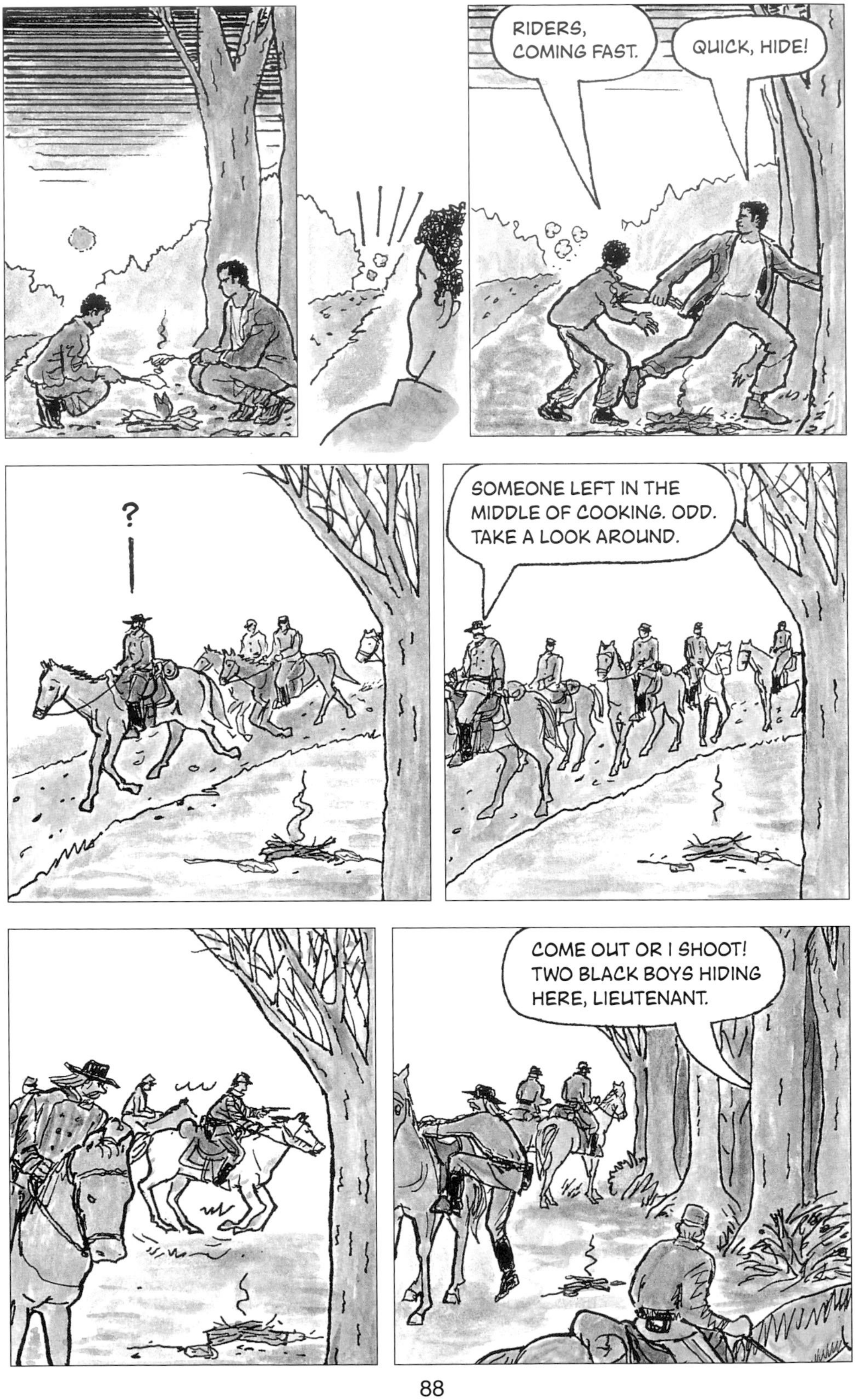
RIDERS, COMING FAST.
QUICK, HIDE!
?
SOMEONE LEFT IN THE MIDDLE OF COOKING. ODD. TAKE A LOOK AROUND.
COME OUT OR I SHOOT! TWO BLACK BOYS HIDING HERE, LIEUTENANT.

91

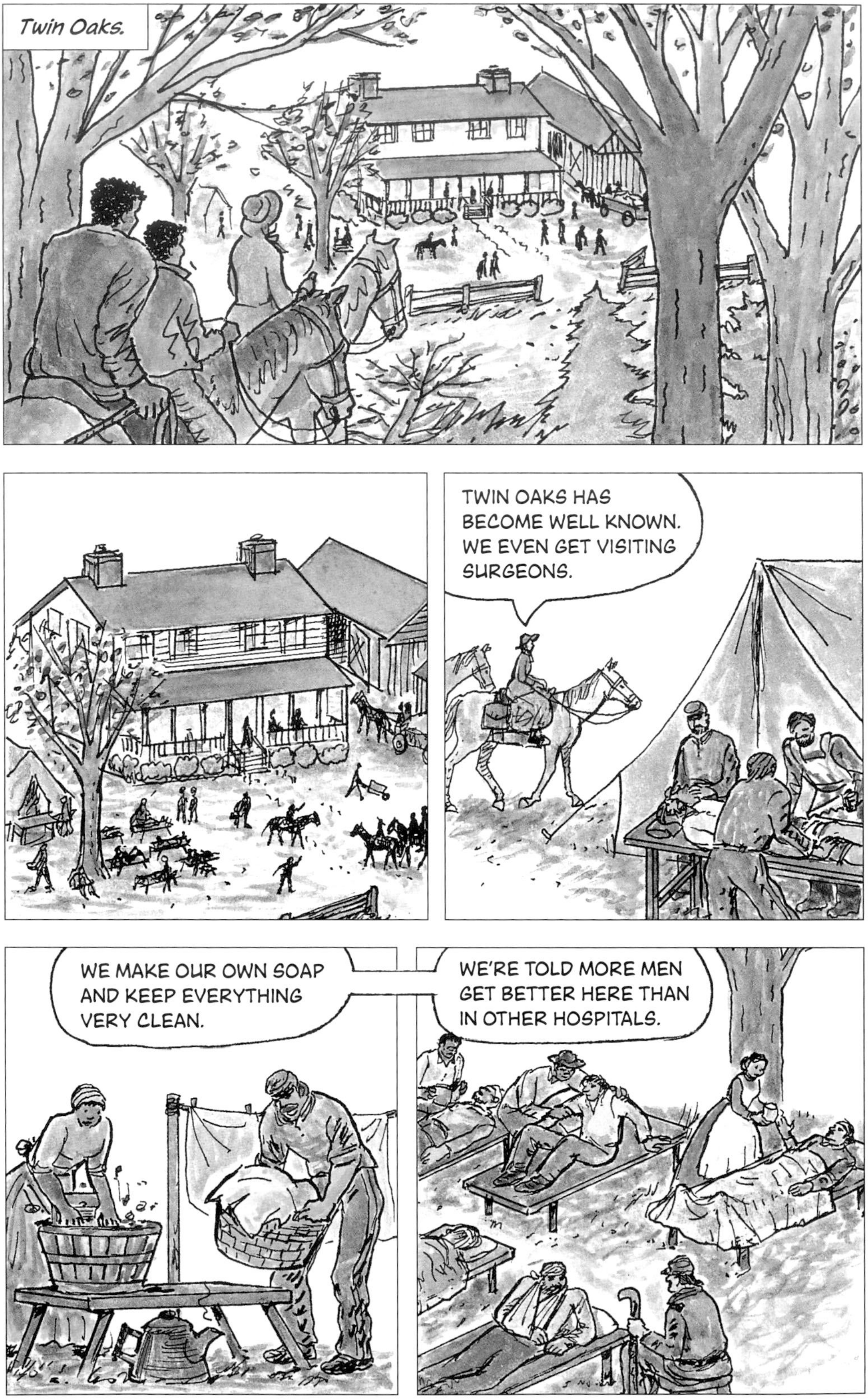
Twin Oaks.
TWIN OAKS HAS BECOME WELL KNOWN. WE EVEN GET VISITING SURGEONS.
WE MAKE OUR OWN SOAP AND KEEP EVERYTHING VERY CLEAN.
WE'RE TOLD MORE MEN GET BETTER HERE THAN IN OTHER HOSPITALS.

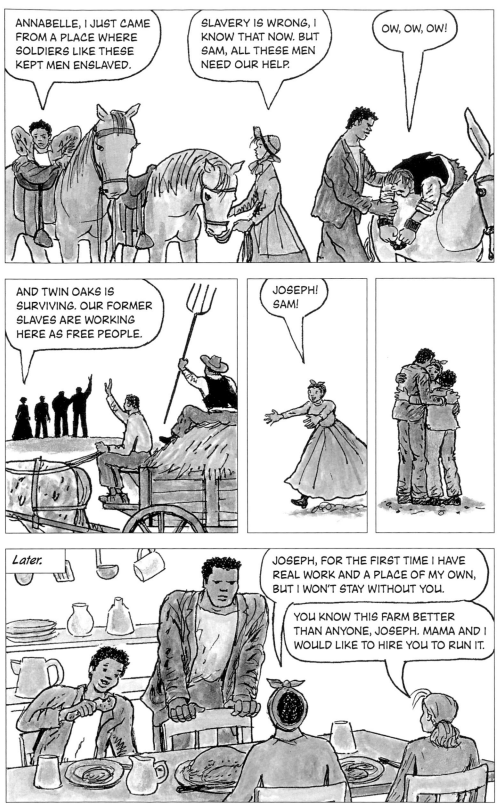

On April 27, the Union offensive, led by General Joseph Hooker, begins. By May 6, with the help of his brilliant general Stonewall Jackson, General Lee has outsmarted Hooker and chased him back across the river. This becomes known as the Battle of Chancellorsville—and Lee's most perfect victory.

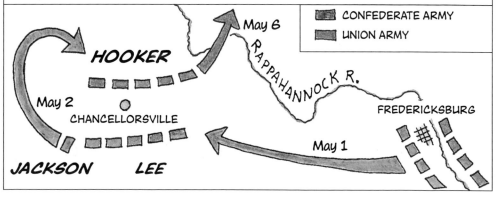

CHAPTER 10

As the war continues, the balance of power begins to shift to the North. The Union Army has more men and supplies, and its ranks are growing with the entry of African American soldiers.

100

Mae recounts Sam's adventures.

Annabelle describes life at Twin Oaks.

108

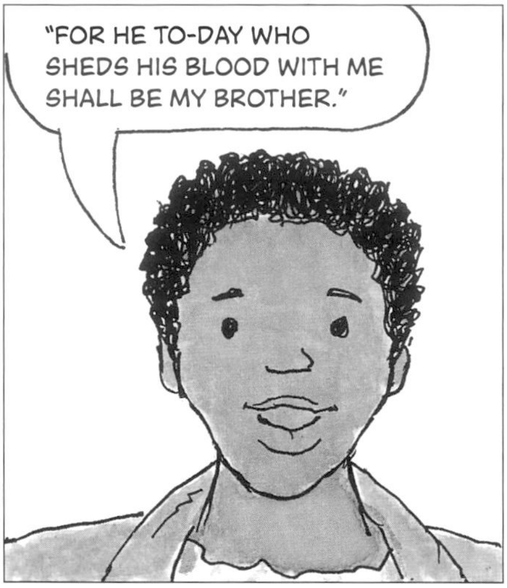
"FOR HE TO-DAY WHO SHEDS HIS BLOOD WITH ME SHALL BE MY BROTHER."

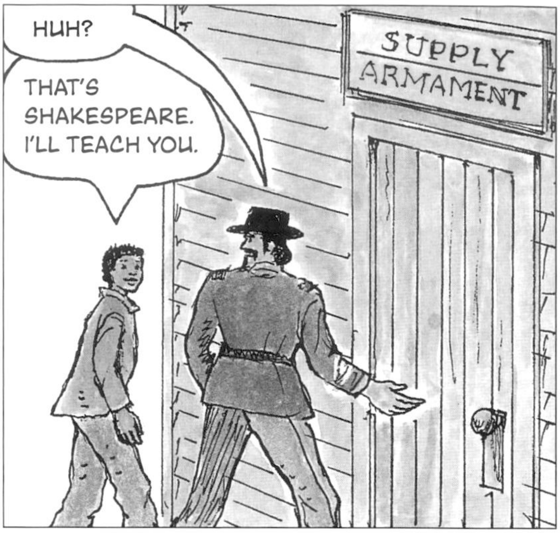
HUH?
THAT'S SHAKESPEARE. I'LL TEACH YOU.
SUPPLY ARMAMENT

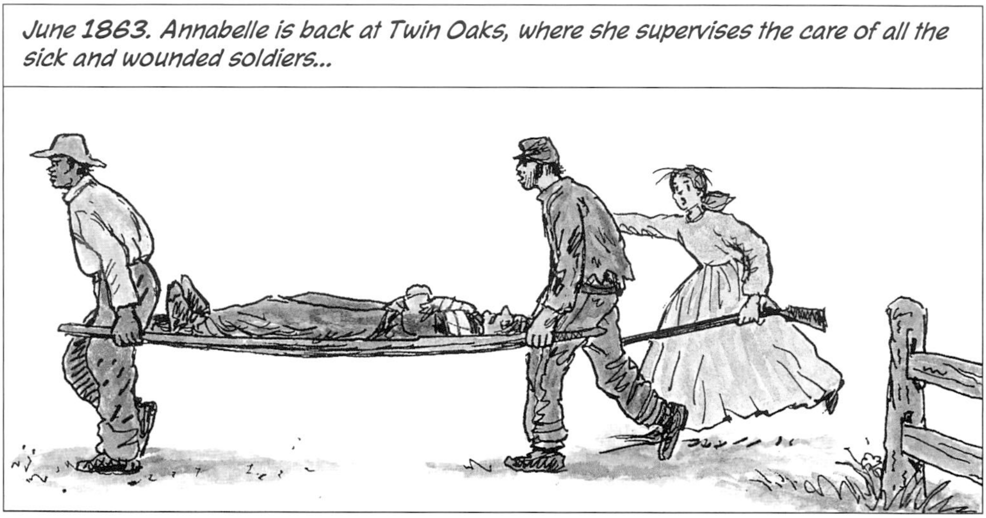
June 1863. Annabelle is back at Twin Oaks, where she supervises the care of all the sick and wounded soldiers...

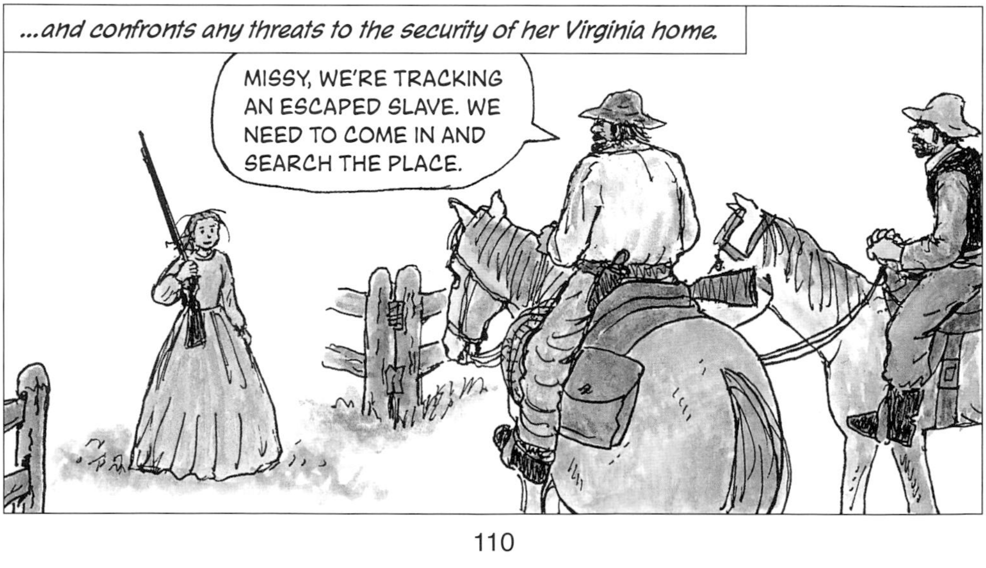
...and confronts any threats to the security of her Virginia home.
MISSY, WE'RE TRACKING AN ESCAPED SLAVE. WE NEED TO COME IN AND SEARCH THE PLACE.

Sam takes his place among the first United States Colored Troops, who quickly prove their courage and willingness to fight.

EPILOGUE

IN WHICH WE LEARN WHAT'S FACT
AND WHAT'S FICTION

CHAPTER 1

Sam, Annabelle, Mae, and Joseph are fictional, but...

* The children of house slaves often did grow up alongside the owner's children on a plantation. Young slaves might work around the plantation house until they were old enough to work in the fields.

* The Bible and the works of Shakespeare were familiar books in Southern homes, so if a slave had the chance and the courage to learn to read (even though it was forbidden), it's possible that they would have read these books.

* Courageous plantation slaves and sympathetic whites *did* help runaway slaves get to freedom.

CHAPTER 2

The actions of the slave hunter and Twist's threat to sell Sam may seem terribly unfair, but...

* Slave hunters did work throughout the South hunting down runaways for reward money. Many turned to trickery—ripping up slaves' identification papers or kidnapping—to grab a profit on the slaves, who had no way to defend themselves.

* One of the greatest punishments slaves suffered was to have their families broken up and family members sold away to distant states.

CHAPTER 3

Sam tells Annabelle, "My father can be free now," but would he really be "free"?

* With the Second Confiscation Act, Union Army officers were no longer obligated to return runaway slaves to their owners. Technically, these runaways were considered captured property, but in reality, upon entering Union territory they were free.

CHAPTER 4

President Lincoln's Emancipation Proclamation declared that slaves in Confederate states were free, but...

*   While Lincoln believed that slavery was wrong, the purpose of the proclamation was really to cause trouble in the South by encouraging more slaves to run. (It said nothing about slaves in the North.) Slavery wasn't officially abolished in the United States until the Thirteenth Amendment to the Constitution was adopted after the war, in December 1865. Nevertheless, despite its limitations, the Emancipation Proclamation seemed to many African Americans the first step toward true freedom, and Lincoln is considered the president who freed the slaves.

CHAPTER 5

Zeke Jefferson didn't really exist, but...

*   The character of Zeke was partially inspired by the real-life Thomas Morris Chester, the only African American reporter for a major newspaper during the Civil War.

*   With the invention of the telegraph—and because the fighting was taking place on our own soil—the Civil War was the first war that could be reported immediately from the battlefield by reporters, artists, and, for the first time, photographers, all of whom competed for "scoops."

The characters Sam meets at Camp Barker are fictional, but...

*   Camp Barker was a real contraband camp, located in northwest Washington City (Washington, DC). Abraham Lincoln was reported to have visited it on his way to his country home outside the city. Today, in the neighborhood of the former Camp Barker stands the African American Civil War Memorial, honoring the African American soldiers who fought for the North during the war.

CHAPTER 6

It may seem unusual that Twin Oaks becomes a hospital, but...

*   Because the fighting ranged everywhere throughout the South and there were so many wounded, private homes were often turned into temporary

hospitals. While it was less common, some hospitals in both the North and the South cared for wounded men from both sides.

* During the Civil War, disease, amputation, and infection killed far more men than bullets did.

CHAPTER 7

Clara Barton never visited the fictional Twin Oaks, but...

* In real life, Clara Barton was the first female nurse to demand to serve on the American battlefields, and she was indeed at the Battle of Fredericksburg. After the war, she went on to establish the American Red Cross.

* Clara Barton talks about a Confederate soldier who risked his life to give water to Union soldiers. There's a statue to this soldier, Sgt. Richard Kirkland, called "The Angel of Marye's Heights," at the Fredericksburg and Spotsylvania National Military Park, in Virginia.

Sam didn't really meet President Lincoln or his son or his bickering advisers at Camp Barker, but...

* Thomas (Tad) was the youngest of Lincoln's four sons. Sadly, Tad died at age eighteen. In fact, only Robert Todd Lincoln, the oldest, made it to adulthood. Edward, the second son, died before his fourth birthday; William (Willie) died at age eleven.

* Unlike many politicians who surround themselves with advisers who agree with them, Lincoln purposely appointed to his cabinet men whose opinions differed from his own—not to mention from one another's.

* It's true that Abraham Lincoln's favorite Shakespeare play was *Macbeth*: "I think nothing equals *Macbeth*," he once said.

CHAPTER 8

Captain K.O. Kelly, Sergeant Bragg, and their mission with Sam are all fictional, but...

* This kind of skirmish may well have happened during the winter of 1862–63 while the Union and Confederate armies were camped on either side of the Rappahannock River.

* At this time (late 1862), African Americans *were* allowed to enlist in the Union Army in noncombat jobs such as cook or scout. But it was extremely dangerous for former slaves to be caught in the South working for the Union. The Confederate Congress stated that any African American soldier or any white officer commanding black soldiers would be severely punished—or even executed.

Joseph couldn't have known what would happen after the war, but...

* He was right that the struggle for equality would last long after the war was over. The Thirteenth Amendment abolished slavery in 1865, but it took another hundred years before the Civil Rights Act outlawed racial discrimination in 1964. And even though we elected an African American president in 2008, this country still struggles to achieve true equality of the races.

CHAPTER 9

In our fictional story, slaves at Twin Oaks are set free and then hired to work for pay.

* In reality, after the war, plantation owners made deals with former slaves to work their land in return for a share of the profits. The system was called sharecropping—but was almost always an unfair arrangement for the freedmen because the plantation owners rarely passed along any of the profits to the workers.

CHAPTER 10

When Zeke says that he thinks General Lee's next battle "will be one for the history books"...

* He's talking about what will become known as the Battle of Gettysburg, in Pennsylvania—Lee's failed attempt to carry the fight to the North. This was later the site of Lincoln's famous Gettysburg Address, in which he emphasized the importance of equality for all.

Annabelle and Mae didn't really meet with President Lincoln, but...

* It's true that Abraham Lincoln set aside times during the week to speak with ordinary people, who would line up outside the White House for the chance to meet with their president.

* Lincoln really was unhappy with Northern general Joseph Hooker. Although he was known as "Fighting Joe," when he had the advantage over Lee at the Battle of Chancellorsville, Hooker suddenly ordered his troops to retreat and take a defensive position, handing Lee the victory.

• • •

On May 22, 1863, the Bureau of Colored Troops was established. All African American soldiers in the Union Army were now officially designated "U.S. Colored Troops." Despite unequal pay and poor equipment compared to white soldiers, these men fought with courage and tenacity and helped the North win the war. The Civil War continued until April 9, 1865, when Southern general Robert E. Lee surrendered to Union general Ulysses S. Grant at Appomattox Court House, Virginia. Six days later, President Lincoln was assassinated at Ford's Theatre in Washington City, by John Wilkes Booth.

Abraham Lincoln was hated by some, beloved by many, and is now considered one of our greatest presidents. His enduring legacy was to bring about the end of slavery, to hold this country together, and to give us a vision of "a more perfect Union."

ACKNOWLEDGMENTS

It sometimes seemed to us that there are more experts on the Civil War than on any other war in history. We were not among them when we started this project. The following people generously offered their time and their extraordinary knowledge as we researched *Fight for Freedom*. If there are any errors in this book, they are ours.

Will Allison, Pamplin Historical Park, Petersburg, Virginia; Stan Brimberg, Bank Street School, New York City; Spencer R. Crew, George Mason University, and Sandra P. Crew, educator; Rim Gardner, Meadow Farm Museum, Glen Allen, Virginia; John Hennessy, Fredericksburg and Spotsylvania National Military Park, Virginia; Hugh Mercer Apothecary, Fredericksburg, Virginia; Hari Jones, African American Civil War Museum, Washington, DC; Kathleen Lang, Monticello, Charlottesville, Virginia; James A. Percoco, historian and educator; Ron Soodalter, historian; Robert K. Sutton, PhD, National Park Service, Washington, DC; Alex Tillen and Gerry Kester, Frontier Culture Museum, Staunton, Virginia; Yohuru Williams, PhD, Fairfield University, Fairfield, Connecticut.

And the following people helped us in many other ways as we brought the book to fruition: Katie and Matthew Cecconi, Malcolm Liu, Kenneth Mack (map), Margaret Miller (our editor), Marsha Miller, the Milonovich family (Katy, Greg, Megan, Thomas, and Ryan), Gary Morris (our agent), Dr. J. Ronald Rich (neurosurgeon, for enabling Stan to draw without pain), Mariana Serra (graphic design), Richard Shapiro, and Annie Taylor (for fine blacking work on the illustrations).